THE BELLS OF SAN JUAN

*Also by Alan LeMay
in Large Print:*

Painted Ponies
Spanish Crossing

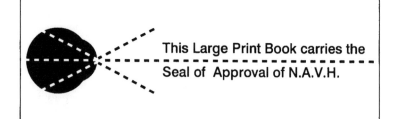

THE BELLS OF SAN JUAN

Western Stories

ALAN LeMAY

Thorndike Press • Waterville, Maine

Published in 2002 by arrangement with Golden West
Literary Agency.

Thorndike Press Large Print Western Series.

The tree indicium is a trademark of Thorndike Press.

The text of this Large Print edition is unabridged.
Other aspects of the book may vary from the original edition.

Set in 16 pt. Plantin by Myrna S. Raven.

Printed in the United States on permanent paper.

Library of Congress Cataloging-in-Publication Data

LeMay, Alan, 1899–1964.
    The bells of San Juan : western stories / Alan LeMay.
      p. cm.
    Contents: The little kid — Lawman's debt — Gray rider
— Trail driver's luck — The loan of a gun — Eyes of
doom — Tombstone's daughter — Star on his heart —
The battle of Gunsmoke Lode — The braver thing —
Sundown corral — The bells of San Juan.
    ISBN 0-7862-2755-9 (lg. print : hc : alk. paper)
    1. Western stories. 2. Large type books. I. Title.
PS3523.E513 A6 2002
    813′.52—dc21   2001042146

TABLE OF CONTENTS

FOREWORD

Alan LeMay, my father, told me that he was not a born writer. He claimed he had to work at it, and he did, twenty-four hours a day. When he wasn't dictating, typing, or making notes on a yellow legal tablet, he was working in his mind. That ability enabled him to pursue a lot of activities without abandoning his current writing project. I learned at an early age to be patient when waiting for an answer to a question. It was as if he had to finish what he was working on before he could reply.

Not content simply to research the events and locales in his stories, he insisted on first-hand information about everything. When he wrote about the South, we moved to New Orleans. In 1929, when he wanted to know more about the West, we took Route 66 from Illinois to California. Although I was only three years old, I remember some of that trip because he made up stories we became a part of. It was fun playing Gypsy, but I didn't like being bedded down alone in the middle of the desert on a very dark night while my parents tried to get our car back on the road. Daddy had pulled off the narrow two-lane highway to get a better look at the giant saguaro cactus by starlight, and our car got stuck in the sand.

But living in the environment of his stories and seeing things first-hand wasn't enough. He experienced as much as he could himself. Learning to fly when he wrote about planes, as well as riding bronchos and being with cowhands and ranchers when he wrote Westerns, gave his writing the veracity it would be hard to achieve any other way. He knew precisely how it felt to be bucked off a horse because it happened to him when he tried broncho-busting.

However, some experiences he didn't ask for. He learned the result of financial failure early in his career when there'd been only carrots for dinner. He hated carrots. He told me he'd tried to switch plates with the dog, but the dog had refused. Perhaps that incident showed him the practical reasons a rancher had to get his beeves to market, and it may be another reason he worked such long hours.

Outside his study, a two-room redwood building down the hill from our home, he built a wooden barrel-like structure at the right height for the body of a horse. He cinched an old Western saddle on it and practiced swinging into the seat without putting his foot in the stirrup as cowboys do in movies. Sometimes he sat in that saddle and swung his horsehair lariat to rope a post some distance away. He knew first-hand how it felt to miss, and the satisfaction of successfully lassoing a dogie before he tried it on a real calf.

Daddy wanted my brother Dan and me to love riding as much as he did. When I was about seven, he gave me a white-faced horse named Lady Buck and announced one afternoon that I was going to learn to ride at a canter. We went to an open field, and he quirted Lady. In panic, I dropped the reins. Since we were galloping toward a steep road out at the end of the field, he shouted: "Dismount! Drop and roll!" I tried to obey, but my left foot caught in the stirrup. With one hand on the pommel and one clutching Lady's mane, I bounced against the horse's side until my shoe came off and I fell to the ground, hitting my head on a rock. Daddy was very upset that he hadn't been able to rescue me. His fresh-broke gelding, Wildfire, had picked that precise moment to go into a bucking fit.

Nevertheless, in true cowboy fashion, he made me get back on my horse and ride her home. In later years, when he related this incident, he emphasized the impending disaster of my riding off the cliff-like drop at the end of the field and his frustration at not being able to save me.

Most of the stories in *The Bells of San Juan* were written before I could read. "The Little Kid" I remember very well. Daddy and Dan and I were living with Grandfather and Grandmother LeMay, the year after my parents' divorce, and he hadn't been on a regular work schedule. However, one evening after supper he closed the door of his room, and I heard the sound of his typewriter until I fell asleep. In the morning he let me read "The Little Kid." The story touched me deeply.

It had a profound impact on another reader as well. After "The Little Kid" was published in *Collier's* magazine, Daddy received a letter from a man who thanked him profusely for writing the story. He said that a similar, almost unbelievable, thing had happened to him as a child, and he'd just about decided it was his own fantasy — until he read my father's story.

Daddy's involvement in writing Westerns carried over into our everyday lives. He always wore cowboy boots, and, when he needed a hat, he wore a tan Stetson. He sang Dan and me to sleep with cattle-quieting lullabies such as "Ragtime Cowboy Joe," "The Streets of Laredo," and "Red River Valley." And he insisted that the only way to cook a steak was blood rare. This all may have been part of total immersion in the subject of his stories, but I believe he thoroughly enjoyed his life style.

My father may not have been a born writer, but he learned his craft with an enthusiasm and sensitivity that could only be called a gift for storytelling. His adventure tales truly capture the spirit of the West while his style, almost poetic at times, remains strictly Alan LeMay.

Jody LeMay Newlove
Pollock Pines, California

THE LITTLE KID

Davy Catlin never knew his mother; she died only a little while after he was born. He knew his father, though, as few boys ever know their fathers, for Tom Catlin gave to his little son all the love he had had for the woman he had lost.

By the time Davy was ten none of the things had happened to him that pessimists had said would happen. He rode the bed wagon, and slept in the same blanket roll with his dad. He had a wonderful time.

Then somewhere far to the north, in the flood waters of a nameless stream, Tom Catlin's Big Red missed his footing in a swirling ford, and over horse and man rolled the resistless press of the plunging, half-swimming cattle. As long as he lived, Ethan, Tom's brother, never forgot that instant's desperate strike-pawing of the down pony, that awful, swift-pushing drift of hundreds of tons of floundering beef.

Ethan explained it to Davy himself, when he got back. Davy was a tall little boy by then, with brown eyes bigger than his face, and sandy hair that straggled straight down over his forehead. Ethan stood before him, as he would stand before a man, and did the best he could. It was mighty hard for Ethan; the sweat was standing out on his face before he was through. The little boy understood better than most would have. He'd seen a good deal, and knew what had happened all right. His uncle thought he took it right well.

But Davy went and hid himself. And as quietly as he could, but unrestrainedly, he sobbed his whole heart out.

Ethan Catlin was starting out again on the last drive of the year. He went and said good bye to Davy, and Davy pretended to say good bye. The boy waited until the cattle — a Circle Slash herd — were thrown out on the trail and well strung out. Then he went home and saddled and packed Blue Baldy. Blue Baldy had been his dad's own cut horse once, but that was quite a piece of time back. Baldy was upward of twenty years old, and kind of pumpkin-shaped by now.

Davy and Blue Baldy overtook the herd one day out. When ordered to explain himself, he said that he guessed it was up to him to get to work and amount to something,

13

now that his dad was gone. That was false, though. Davy didn't want to tell his real reason. The truth was that in the bottom of his heart he couldn't handle the idea that his dad was wholly gone, not in the world any more. He had to get up there to where his dad last was. As if he could somehow find some part of Tom Catlin there yet, in the wind, in the grass — Davy could not have explained it, even to himself. But he somehow just had to get up that northward trail to Dodge.

Ethan promised himself to take his brother's place, as well as he could. Ethan, leather-faced and iron-eyed from his saddle years, was all right. He wasn't Dad. Nobody could ever be Dad. . . .

Davy fitted in all right — pulled his weight. Without being told, he took over most of the day-wrangling.

So they got up the trail into cold, and rain, and early-closing winter, and once more the streams were unnaturally high, as in the spring before, and the cattle fought the crossings. All through the second month Davy was watching those crossings. He was a savvy kid, and he was pretty sure they wouldn't show him the place where his dad went down. But he thought he would know it when they came to it. Somehow he would just know.

14

And then they came to the night of the fog stampede. That night was famous for a long time. Nobody that got through it ever forgot it.

There had been a fall of snow, unseasonably early, then a swift melt, with deep going underfoot, and higher crossings. Nobody had allowed for the heavy, dripping fog that came on them that night — a rare, nearly unheard-of thing for that country.

The three thousand head of Circle Slash steers got mighty superstitious over it; even before sundown they were going on the moan. The thick blanket that closed down with the dark was pretty weird, all right.

Ethan Catlin strengthened his night guard until two thirds of his boys rode at once. They circled the herd at a jog, singing, which sometimes keeps cattle from fretting too much over other things. The boys by the fire brought tight-cinched ponies right up to their bedrolls; some dozed with the reins in their hands.

The herd was fairly steady until about eleven o'clock, and then it went, without any extra warning. There was a general, swiftly building drift of movement all over the vast bedding ground, and a rising terrible rumble, through which laced the — *"Yip-whoop!"* — of the cowboys and the suddenly loosed rattle of their guns as they frantically tried a quick stop. It was the dreaded fog stampede.

Ethan Catlin shouted: "*Hup,* boys!" He vaulted into his saddle, and horses and men were swallowed instantly by the night and the rumbling plain. He didn't need to holler; the others were up just as soon.

And the little kid — Davy had Baldy all ready. He scrambled into the saddle and bolted after the others. He sat in behind Jess McBride, whom he knew by the glimpsed gray quarters of his pony as it left the fire circle.

There was a long, hard run then. Davy couldn't see Jess, but Blue Baldy knew what he was doing. Baldy stretched everything to keep his nose to the tail of that gray. Jess got them out in front, in the end.

Both youngster and old horse were blowing hard by the time Davy knew they were in front. He could tell they were in the lead of the stampede now because, whenever Baldy slacked, the rumbling roar behind them closed up, but held even again when Baldy reached out hard and pulled. Davy yelled with everything he had, and rode, trying like the rest to turn the lead cattle, hopeless as it was.

Then presently he didn't know where Jess

was any more. He could still hear the thin long war-yells of the cowboys, but he couldn't tell where, they were so smothered by that earth-shaking thunder behind.

Then pretty soon he couldn't hear the others at all, but only that increasing rumble of the earth, and the *snap* of the clashing horns. Baldy was laboring now, and Davy knew he had done enough. He began to rein to the left, to get out of it. He was hoping with all his heart that he had done his part, that his dad would have been proud, if he could have known.

Then, as he reined to the left, the thunder was at the left of him, and he had to turn back, to try for the other side, although the other side was a long way off. Suddenly he knew he couldn't do that, either. He knew this country, some. Up ahead, to the right especially, lay the Chickasaw Brakes, a tangle of square-cut washes, eight to twenty feet deep, lacing the flat ground. A trail-smart man might have got through there in front of a stampede by daylight. No man that lived could do it at night — not this blind night.

A sick terror swept the little kid. The herd was behind them, and at the sides, cupping them in, and the cruel brakes were ahead. In a few more minutes poor Baldy would be

17

down in some God-forsaken wash, with cattle pouring in on top, broken and bawling, until the wash was full.

And they were all alone, terribly alone. Davy's free hand went up to cover his open mouth, and the tears jumped from his eyes, as he would never have thought they would. After all, he was only a little boy. And he knew that he was gone.

He whimpered — "Oh, God . . . oh, God. . . ." — and closed his eyes against that evil blank blackness.

Then suddenly a horse rushed up beside Blue Baldy. Somehow, even in that great earth-growl, Davy could make out that hard new hammer of fast hoofs. There was a great, slamming stride to this horse that came up, for all the world like Big Red, the horse that went down with Dad in the crossing, and no other.

A voice spoke, clear and strong, close to him, and even through all that noise Davy could hear it very plain: "Steady, Davy . . . steady, boy!"

It was his father's voice, the first voice he could remember in his life, and the last he would ever forget. And, as he turned to look, Davy could see his father, a little better, much better, than he could see Blue Baldy. No mistaking that tall, solid frame, in any dark.

Davy cried out — "Dad!" — in a great agony of joy and relief, and he leaned out to touch his father. Only, the drift of the racing ponies carried them a little apart, so he couldn't reach him.

His father said: "Swing left, Davy . . . swing left hard! We need to outreach the herd's left point!"

"Dad, they're ahead of us there! Can Baldy make it?"

The answer came strong and deep: "Sure, Baldy can make it! Baldy's got to make it! Best horse in the country. Give him steel!"

So Davy spurred Baldy, and the old horse picked up.

"Throw left here, quick!" his father told him. "It's the bow of the first coulée."

Davy couldn't see how he knew — didn't need to see. He swung sharp left. Immediately, to the right of them, there was a ghastly bawling, and the crash of broken carcasses, as some of the herd went over the drop, where Baldy would have dropped, too, if they hadn't turned.

"Pick up Baldy's head, light and smooth," Dad said. "We can cross this arroyo here. Hold up his head and jump him in!"

Davy got hold of Baldy's head, and down they went over a six-foot drop, but Baldy's old knees held up, and they handled it.

"Now up!" And up and out they went with a bound and a scramble, and were running on.

"Now left again, and give him hell! That left horn of the herd . . . we've got to take it now! Not much room left . . . but just enough!"

"Yes, Dad!" He spurred, and Baldy tried, and pulled up a little. Not enough, though. A bit of froth whipped back and caught Davy in the mouth. He could taste blood in it. The old horse was almost done.

"The romal, Davy. The romal! Pour the leather to him!"

That big, beloved ringing voice seemed to lift old Baldy better than the lash, as Davy hit Baldy. Baldy laid into it with everything he had.

"Hard, Davy boy! Cut him in two!"

The little kid was whipping the pony as hard as he could. But a lurch was coming into Baldy's stride; he slacked and faltered. Davy saw he wasn't going to make it through. "Dad! He can't make it! Dad . . . Dad! Pick me up! Baldy's gone!"

At that, just for that one moment, uncertainty came into his father's voice. It was almost the only time Davy ever heard it there. "Why, Son . . . why, Son. . . ." Then once more his father's voice rose powerful and clear: "You, Baldy!" Davy saw his father's quirt stripe Baldy's rump, and there was the flicker of blue lightning in the lash. But it was the voice that lifted the pony, more than the quirt — the voice that the pony must have remembered from long ago: *"You, Baldy!"* That great, vibrant voice could have lifted any horse, anywhere; it could have lifted a hill, or a tree.

And Blue Baldy answered; he answered as no horse should be able to answer, even if he were young and fresh. They pulled ahead hard, fast, wind screaming in Davy's ears and the fog rime wetting his face.

"Cut through, now! Cut fast through the leaders! Quick! It's the rim!"

"Daddy . . . I can't see!"

"Never mind . . . I've got him. . . ."

Big Red jumped ahead, and Baldy turned short as Davy's father got him by the bit, leading him through. For a minute, invisible thundering shapes were all around them; a horn ripped through Davy's jeans at the knee, but didn't hurt him much.

Then at last they were out of it, clean and clear, and they pulled the ponies down, letting them walk. Davy felt himself crying again, but this time he didn't care. Partly he was crying from fatigue, and partly from relief, but mostly it was from pure happiness that his father was near him again, as he could never have expected him to be. He turned to look at his father; he couldn't see him quite so clearly now, perhaps because of the tears.

His father spoke to him once more, and now his voice was soft and low: "Good ride, fella." His voice was dimmed, too — farther away. But in it was all the love that one man's heart can hold. It flowed into the little kid, into his heart, filling him with warmth, all over. "Good ride, boy . . . you made me mighty proud. . . ."

It was early morning when Davy got back to the fire again. Most of the riders were in by then, those that were ever coming in. Jess McBride was missing, done for in the Chickasaw Brakes, and there were more.

Ethan Catlin was nearly busted up to see Davy come in. They'd given him up, long ago. As Baldy came into the firelight, and stood head down and lip dangling, Davy tumbled out of the saddle, mighty stiff and done up. They stood him by the fire, and got blankets around him, and gave him hell out of sheer relief.

Ethan kept swearing to himself, over and over. "Damnedest thing I ever heard tell. Look at that horn rip in his pants!"

"Look at the rode-out horse," said another. "He sure fitted that old pony to a ride."

"Gosh!" Ethan said. "When I think of that little kid out there all alone. . . ."

Davy said: "I wasn't alone. My father was there. My father was there, on Big Red."

That silenced them, and they looked at him very oddly. "What was that you said?"

"My father came up and rode with me," Davy told them again. "He showed me the way as we came through the brakes. He made my ride for me. It was him that forced Baldy on, when Baldy was played out and done for. And he led Baldy by the cheek strap, right through the leaders of the herd."

They said nothing, only exchanged glances.

"I know what you're thinking," Davy said. "You're thinking that my father is dead. But I know now that he isn't dead. Oh, I know he was killed, and all . . . I savvy that all right. But I mean not really dead. He isn't really dead at all."

There was quiet again. Ethan said: "Sonny, I don't scarcely believe you know what you mean."

Davy said: "I reckon I don't need to know what I mean. Only, I know now I don't ever need to be afeared of nothing no more. Because I know now my father is still a-goin' to side-ride me, when I need him bad. Right when I need him most."

He stood with the blankets over his shoulders, looking into the fire, a tall little boy with brown eyes bigger than his face, and sandy hair uncombed and straggly. And his face was proud, and happy, in the light of the flames.

"I wasn't alone, tonight," Davy said. "I wasn't alone because he was there. And I know he'll always be there when I need him most. Always . . . always. . . ."

LAWMAN'S DEBT

Darkness had set in, and the rain was falling in a steady downpour as Dale Jameson, looking like some misshapen monster out of the past, in his yellow slicker and huge hat, entered the tiny cabin of saplings. He had built it in secret in the midst of a dense clump of spruce against this need.

Here he would stay until the hue and cry had ceased. Then, with beard grown and in the garb of a prospector, he would go west over the divide and eventually reach civilization beyond — unknown, unsought, and unafraid.

He pulled off the slicker, and from his back he unstrapped a canvas bag that was stuffed to overflowing with currency and gold.

Quickly he built a fire in the tiny fireplace, put on a coffee pot, and spitted a venison steak on a stick before the leaping flames. Then, with shaking hand, he opened the canvas bag and poured a fortune out on the pine-board table. It was a huge pile, and he wondered how so much money could come out of so small a bag.

He had no fear of pursuit. His plan had been well made; it had been cleverly executed, and his trail had been well covered. Caching saddle and bridle and turning his pinto loose near Las Vegas Cañon was a master stroke. No one ever would think of him leaving his horse and going on foot to a hide-out by a path no mounted posse could follow.

Perhaps, even now, the two men in the bank were still bound and gagged and the alarm not yet given. Or at most the word was being passed that the Pioneer State Bank had been robbed by one man, and that a stranger by the name of Brad Kelly was suspected. Who would know that Dale Jameson, the respected son of a prosperous rancher who lived far away, had staged the daring hold-up?

Slowly and deliberately Dale piled up the gleaming yellow coins. Carefully he separated the bills into fives, tens, and twenties. There was a thick pack of one-hundred-dollar bills with the figure **$10,000** stamped on the band around it. Fifty-three thousand, seven hundred, and forty dollars was the total haul. What a tidy sum to wrest from one institution without bloodshed and without the slightest difficulty!

He had slipped through a back door in the afternoon and hid in a closet till the bank was closed, the doors locked, and the curtains drawn. Then, like an avenging demon, he appeared with handkerchief over face and gun in hand. He tied the two men in the bank hand and foot, looted the safe at his leisure, and walked quietly out the back door and away. In the whole community only a few people knew him, and they knew him as Brad Kelly, a cowboy from the Mancos River country.

Jap Heathcote was right. A man was a fool to work all his life when he could so easily take the proceeds of labor away from those who had less brains or smaller courage. Why should a wolf dig for roots when succulent mutton was nearby, guarded by weak and incompetent dogs?

Weak and incompetent dogs!

Dale grimaced slightly at the thought as he fingered the piles of currency and gold. There was one fly in the ointment! The watchdog of this particular fold was neither weak nor incompetent. Dale had passed him on the street two weeks before the hold-up, and his eyes had fallen as the keen glance of the sheriff had met his own. He had suddenly found himself facing his boyhood hero — old Bat Masters of border fame — who was his father's best friend. Frequently Masters had come to the Texas ranch in the old days. He had bounced Dale on his knee and let him hold the big .45 that swung at his side. It was a strange coincidence that Bat Masters should be at the scene of Dale's first crime, and that this terror of outlaws should meet his first defeat at the hands of the boy to whom he had been on a par with Robin Hood and Richard of the Lion Heart.

Masters looked a little older now. His shoulders were a trifle stooped; the long, sweeping mustache was a trifle grizzled; but there was the same fire in the blue eyes, and doubtless there was the same skill in the lightning hand. Yet Dale had won! He had won against this noted guardian of the law, the man who had brought grief to so many who had stood without the pale.

Dale wished that Jap Heathcote could see him and know what he had done, that he had executed the perfect bank robbery, and had committed the perfect crime. As well for Bat Masters to try and catch the lightning playing above the mountain tops as to try to bring Dale Jameson to justice.

The savory odor of coffee and broiling venison roused him from his reverie, and he arose with a sigh. He turned the steak and shifted the coffee pot, shielding his face from the heat of the flames with his hand. The wind had arisen, and the little cabin trembled in spite of its protection from the surrounding trees.

A draught of cold air struck the back of Dale's neck and fanned the flames in the fireplace. The door had blown open. He was not nervous, and he did not turn until the coffee pot was settled where it could simmer instead of boil. Strange that the door should blow open! He must have failed to close it in his haste.

Slowly he turned. Then his eyes grew wide, his jaw dropped, and he stood staring into the round orifice of a six-gun held by a steady hand. Behind it a black and wet slicker gleamed and glistened in the firelight. Above it was a face with a long, grizzled mustache and the keenest of keen, blue eyes.

"Brad Kelly," spoke a calm voice that reminded Dale of the cold steel of edged tools. "I thought so!"

With manacled hands Dale lay on his cot throughout the wild night. He felt a strange comfort in the fact that Bat Masters had not recognized him. It would be easier to endure the long years of prison life if this silent man did not know the one he had taken to justice was the son of his old friend — the boy he had held on his knee.

Thoughts of escape flashed through his mind, but they struggled feebly and died as he looked at this man of iron who was smoking silently as the frail shelter was battered by the wind and rain. The perfect crime and the clever escape had come to a sudden and inglorious end. This stern, relentless guardian of the law had caught him scarcely before he had counted his stolen loot. It was uncanny how quickly Dale had been gathered in.

Mentally he cursed the memory of Jap Heathcote. Dale was a fool to have been attracted and led astray by the dashing outlaw. His father had warned and pleaded and threatened and cajoled, until there came a final, violent quarrel when Dale left the paternal roof and went his own way. Jap Heathcote had died with a bullet between the eyes shortly after his young friend had joined him, and Dale had gone on alone.

Only once did Dale speak, and that was to ask how Masters had trailed him. For some moments the sheriff smoked on without answering. His eyes were on a little, colored picture of a doe and fawn that Dale had tacked on the wall. When he spoke, it was with seeming irrelevance.

"There ain't many people in a county like this," he drawled. "A few ranchers, a few miners, a few prospectors, and a few businessmen make up the whole population. But the county has miles and miles of plains, hills, and mountains. A sheriff wouldn't amount to shucks up here unless he knew a good many things that most people wouldn't notice. Sometimes he learns secrets from prospectors and lion hunters and trappers that go to the most hidden places in the wilds. Sometimes he learns something from those that are much sharper than any human.

"Someone tells the sheriff of a strange young man living above Las Vegas Cañon. One day the sheriff goes up there. He sees a deer that runs on ahead and disappears. Pretty soon it comes dashing back. Something is up ahead . . . either man or animal. Some jays are screaming in a clump of spruce. They settle down and then rise up again and scold. The sheriff knows there is something in that spruce that shouldn't be there. The jays tell him so. Then comes the sound of a hammer.

"The sheriff slips through the trees and sees a young man building a cabin. That's harmless enough, so the sheriff goes away,

31

and the young man is no part the wiser. Later he sees the same young man in town. He looks at him, and the young man drops his eyes. He can't look the law in the face. The sheriff asks about him and learns he is Brad Kelly, occupation unknown . . . supposed to be a cowboy from a Mancos River ranch. A letter from Mancos River says they don't know him. The bank is robbed by a lone man. The description tallies with Brad Kelly who built the little cabin. What's the answer?"

Masters puffed away at his pipe and said no more. Dale lay silently in his misery. What a child he had been when pitted against this machine of the law! How quickly the solution to his perfect crime had been solved! What a fool he was! If he ever got out of this mess. . . . But it was too late now! He had broken the law and must pay the penalty.

Then his thoughts turned to escape. Perhaps even yet there was a chance. Bat Masters had not recognized him. Let him get away and he would be hard to follow. Jap Heathcote had told him: "Never turn yellow if you get caught. Keep your chin up and your mouth shut and ten to one you can crawl out even if they get you behind bars."

In early dawn the two men left the cabin

and started along the path that led down the tortuous decent into Las Vegas Cañon. The rain had ceased, and the wind had gone down, but the clouds hung dark and forbidding above them. Every mountain rill and dry creekbed had become a torrent that plunged and snarled its angry way over the rocks.

Coming out on the rimrock above the cañon, they paused and stared without speaking at the stupendous change that had been wrought by the few hours of heavy rain. Normally Las Vegas River was a clear, small stream that sang and bubbled and tumbled among the boulders. Now it had risen high and was filled with mud and débris. Its dark waters dashed in a wild race for the valley below, churning the brown foam and flinging spray far into the air. The cry of the tortured stream in its travail echoed against the sides of the cañon and reached the men on the rimrock far up against the sky.

Together they slipped and slid down over the wet rocks. It was a dangerous descent for Dale. The handcuffs were still around his wrists, but he would have died rather than ask that they be removed.

An hour later they reached the road at the side of the stream. It continued up the cañon to Las Vegas dam.

Foam and spray dashed over them as they moved down the road. Evidently the dam was full to the brim, and the water was dashing over the spillways. Dale shuddered to think what would happen if the dam should break, and the vast store of irrigation water be loosed upon the valley below.

In a little cavern at the side of the road they came to the sheriff's horse, which had waited patiently for him. Masters had removed the saddle and bridle and thrown his blanket over it.

With Dale in the lead, the sheriff walking behind him and the horse following, they emerged from the cañon into the green valley, dotted thickly with haystacks. For a hundred yards the water was over the road.

Dale looked about him for the slightest chance of escape, but saw none. If he only had his hands free, he might plunge into the stream. It was deep here within a few feet of the road, and he might get away with a long dive and powerful swimming.

On the other side was a thick grove of cottonwood trees, standing in the water. The road ran straight ahead a mile or more, then it rose sharply and continued over the hills to the town.

A fine, cold rain had set in, and the two men splashed through the water and mud with hunched shoulders and bowed heads. In spite of his desperate situation, Dale was filled with admiration for Bat Masters. Nearly sixty years old the sheriff must be, yet no storm was too violent, no test was too severe to prevent him from going forth in the performance of his duty, preventing crime, apprehending the criminal, and enforcing the law. The institutions of established society must be worthwhile, after all, when such men spent their lives upholding them. The fortune that Masters carried in the canvas bag was no more to him than so much wheat. No temptation could be great enough for this man to take one penny of it.

A faint trembling of the earth took Dale's mind abruptly from these thoughts. The horse threw up its head and snorted. It snorted again as a roaring came to their ears that grew steadily louder like a terrific wind approaching though the pines.

"The dam!" cried Bat Masters. "It has gone out!"

Dale's face paled at the thought of the danger that faced them. They were directly in the path of the unleashed flood, too far down the road now to reach the safety of the cañon walls! Trapped!

The sheriff acted quickly. He turned to the horse, slapped it with the flat of his hand. "Get out!" he commanded. "Go!" The terrified animal went dashing toward the hills. "He won't carry double," Masters explained, as he swiftly unlocked the handcuffs and took them from Dale's wrists. "Climb that tree," he ordered. "It may hold. It's each for himself now."

Dale noted the silent fulfillment of the unwritten code of the West that required the sheriff to stay with his prisoner, as he swung into the branches of a big cottonwood. The sheriff might have escaped alone on his horse, but that was not Bat Masters's way.

The roar grew louder. Suddenly a wall of water burst from the mouth of the cañon a mile away. Spreading like some huge, feathered fan, it gushed over the valley.

A white ranch house, with its unpainted barn and corral, was swept away like so much straw. A small herd of cattle disappeared in the plunging foam. Then a five-foot roaring wall of water was upon them.

The tree trembled like a reed as the flood struck, and Dale wondered how anything could stand against the battering ram that had been unloosed against them. On every side was a plunging, seething, pounding sea carrying with it the fruits of destruction.

Huge trees, uprooted and tossed about, swirled by them, turning end over end or riding low in the flood. There were logs and planks and boards, and once Dale saw the roof of a house that had been torn loose like a toy.

A dead steer came to the surface for a moment and swirled around and around before it disappeared in the brown flood. A huge log struck and lodged against their tree, which shook and trembled under the blow.

The sheriff, clinging to a branch on the other side of the trunk, pointed and shouted. Although Dale could not understand all the words, he knew Masters was saying that their tree must go if enough débris piled against that log, and that nothing could live in that roaring hell.

Again the sheriff shouted, and Dale's eyes followed his pointed finger. From the mouth of the cañon burst a second wall of water. Evidently not all of the dam had given way at one time. Masters pulled off his heavy slicker and motioned Dale to do likewise.

Dale watched the widening fringe flung out over the valley. Nearer and nearer it came. Trees that had resisted the first onslaught were going down, uprooted or snapped off like toothpicks before the fury of the flood.

The sheriff held out his hand. Dale gripped it hard. No need for spoken words. Their tree, with the log and swiftly accumulated débris of all kinds, could not stand against the impending blow.

Masters smiled, but Dale could not answer that smile. The sheriff could laugh in the face of death, for he was going out in the performance of his duty — honest and clean. Bat Masters was a man!

Dale felt that he was about to die, and he had ceased to care. He was neither nervous nor afraid. His one regret was that he could not go like Bat Masters.

With a roar like the loosing of a thousand seas, the plunging, surging mass of water was upon them. The cottonwood gave a sickening shudder and leaned slightly out of the perpendicular. The log was torn away and went swinging end over end into the maëlstrom. For a moment Dale hoped. The crest of the flood passed. Perhaps, after all. . . .

Again came that sickening shudder. Then, slowly and steadily, the great tree tipped. It touched the angry water with its lower branches, paused a moment, and then, as though worn out with the long battle, darted down the stream as the last root gave away.

With both arms and both legs wrapped around the branch, Dale struck the water. Even then his hold was almost broken as the foaming flood tore by. His head came above the surface of the stream, and he opened his eyes, surprised to find himself still alive. The branch was steady for a moment, but this was no assurance for the future. He could see trees as large as this one flung about and turned over and over farther out in the stream.

A whirlpool caught them. Dale took a deep breath as he was plunged beneath the surface. Something seemed to tell him to hang on, and he clung to the limb till it seemed his lungs would burst, clung till there was a ringing in his ears, clung till he thought the end had come, and he had descended into the dark and fathomless pit to eternity.

There was a quick heave, and he was flung a yard above the surface of the stream, still clinging to his branch. He glanced across the tree. Bat Masters was no longer there.

The cottonwood was floating broadside down the river now, and Dale noticed a foot or more of seemingly still water following along behind the big trunk beneath. Into this still place came a head. It floated a moment and then sank slowly.

Scarcely realizing what he was doing, Dale reached down and grasped the long hair. Slowly he lifted, and the face of Bat Masters came into view. It was a pitiful face now with its long, dripping mustache. It was white and drawn, and the old fire had gone out of the half-closed eyes.

The cottonwood had stopped its mad whirling and was floating steadily. Dale knew that the worst of the flood was over. If he could hang on a few minutes longer, he might yet cheat the death that was reaching for him with dripping hands.

Again the tree turned. Loosing his hold, Dale dropped into the water, seized another branch with his right hand, and passed his left arm around the sheriff. He could see that they were drifting toward the shore, away from the violent middle of the stream. There was hope, if Dale could hang on. A small log dashed against him, knocking the breath from him and nearly causing him to lose his hold.

He looked at the face beside him. The eyes were wide open now, and Dale knew the sheriff was alive and conscious. There was a surge as they sped down a little rapid, and the branch was nearly torn from Dale's grasp. The strain upon hand and arm was terrific.

"Can you help me hang on?" he shouted.

The head moved slightly from side to side, and the eyes closed.

The run down the rapid had driven the tree farther toward the shore. Slower and slower it moved. Dale was sure that the flood must be receding rapidly; already it seemed that a thousand lakes as big as Las Vegas had swept past them.

Suddenly the tree halted. It moved again, trembled, and then came to a full stop. Dale's feet touched bottom a moment and then were lifted by the current.

The tree moved again in little jerks, and then the branches caught, and the trunk swung downstream. Again Dale touched the bottom, and this time he stood firm!

The flood had spent its force. A few minutes later the exhausted Dale carried the limp body of the sheriff to solid ground. A hasty examination showed a cut on the head, a badly bruised wrist, and the right leg, hanging limp and twisted. Cutting away the trouser leg, Dale found the limb broken above the knee. The shattered bone showed in a white lump.

"Are you badly hurt?" Dale asked, and realized as he spoke how idiotic his question was.

There was no answer. The blue eyes were

open and upon him, and Dale was sure that Masters was conscious. He pulled off his scarf and bound the scalp wound, wondering if putting on a wet and muddy bandage was the proper thing to do.

The gleam of handcuffs in the sheriff's pocket brought him to a sudden realization of his opportunity. Dale looked about him, wondering vaguely if the coast was clear for him.

Far away two men on horses topped a hill and disappeared in a little valley as they rode toward the stream. In all the soggy wasteland that the flood had left behind it, no other living being was in sight.

The words of Jap Heathcote came to Dale with double force: "Never turn yellow if you get caught. Keep your chin up and your mouth shut and ten to one you can crawl out even if they get you behind bars."

Jap Heathcote was right! Dale had kept his chin up and his mouth shut, and now he could escape after being in the hands of Bat Masters, the famous hunter of men.

With shaking hands, Dale unstrapped the canvas bag that Masters had carried through the jaws of death, and pulled the sheriff's gun from its holster. The blue eyes were upon him, and the old fire was returning, but there was no word and no sign from the injured man.

Dale was very tired, yet the prospect of escape with the stolen fortune gave him new life and new strength. He glanced at the still swollen stream, shuddered, wondered that he had come out alive and uninjured from it. Then, with long strides, he ascended the slope that bordered the valley.

Again the horsemen rode into view. They were headed far to the right, and there was no danger from them. Dale paused and looked back at Bat Masters who was lying motionless in a pathetic heap. This relentless, merciless instrument of the law could not follow him now. As for the rest of the community — they would have enough to do in searching for their dead. Dale would get away safely with the wet, sodden loot that was strapped to his back.

The sheriff moved. Slowly and painfully he struggled to one knee and tried to drag himself over the ground. Then he sank down and lay still.

Dale knew he would die there alone, unless he was rescued, and who could find him amidst those miles of wreckage piled high in the wake of the flood? The horsemen were still in sight, but they were traveling rapidly and would not come within a mile of the injured sheriff.

Dale reached and touched the canvas bag,

now on his back again. Ahead lay comfort and plenty. Behind lay years of prison life. Then, hardly knowing what he did, he shouted loudly! The horsemen rode on. Dale lifted his voice again and again in a call that carried far over the open range.

The horsemen stopped. Still in the grip of an urge he could not name, Dale frantically waved his hand. Presently he saw an answering signal, and the two men rode toward him.

A moment later he was at Bat Masters's side. The sheriff lay in a twisted heap, but his keen blue eyes were upon Dale.

Dale threw the canvas bag down beside him, and shoved the big .45 back in its holster. Then he held out his hands for the handcuffs, and smiled into the blue eyes.

"I've come back, Sheriff," he said calmly. "I'll take my medicine and then go straight as long as I live."

"Yeah," answered Masters, and his voice startled Dale coming from one so long silent. "I thought that was what you would do. Sometimes it's hard to go straight, son, a good many people fail when the pinch comes, but, after all, it's the easy way."

He made no movement to put on the handcuffs. Dale moved him to a more comfortable position, and then sat by his side till

44

the men rode up. Dale did not know them.

"Hyah, Sheriff?" greeted one. "Are you hurt?"

"Yes. Busted leg. Put on a couple of splints and I can make it to town on a horse."

The eyes of one of the men fell on the canvas bag as he dismounted.

"What's this?" he asked.

"The money stolen from the bank," the sheriff answered.

"Great Scott, you got him, did you?"

Masters nodded.

"And is this the fellow that . . . that . . . ?"

The keen eyes of the sheriff looked into Dale's young face. It was weary and drawn and showed the strain of the past few hours. "I caught Brad Kelly and got back the money," Masters said. "Then the flood came, and he . . . he's out there, drowned. We never will see Brad Kelly again. This young fellow came along and saved my life at the risk of his own. Men, I want you to meet Dale Jameson, the son of the best and truest friend I ever had . . . and Dale's a chip off the old block. I'm proud to be numbered among his friends."

And Bat Masters, relentless scourge of the outlaw, reached out and took Dale's hand in a firm grasp.

GRAY RIDER

1

"Range Law"

The rolling land was covered with the faint green of new grama grass that seemed struggling hopelessly for existence in the midst of a burned prairie. A small clump of willows surrounded a water hole that should have been filled to the brim, but, in the rainless land, it had sunk to a slime-covered sink.

Near the water hole stood a man wearing a huge hat, bull-leather, batwing chaps, a blue shirt, and leather vest. A short distance from him a calf lay tied. A branding iron slowly heated in a fire of sticks and dry cow chips. The man moved the iron from time to time, heaping fuel over it and fanning the flames with his hat. Finally he took it from the fire and applied it, sizzling, to the flank of the calf that bawled with the pain. A

Double Q was burned on the tender hide.

The man untied the calf, and it dashed away toward a dozen of its fellows on the other side of the water hole. As he turned toward his horse, there came a sharp, vicious *hum* in the air. He threw up his arms, turned half around. His knees buckled under him, and he fell face downward.

A crow flew overhead, cawing harshly. The small herd of cows and calves moved slowly away. The horse continued to crop the short grass close to its silent master.

The distorted red rim of the sun disappeared slowly beneath the dust-covered prairie horizon. Six men on horses were riding toward the foothills that rose, sharp and jagged, above a stream that trickled bravely through the burned plain. A straggling grove of cottonwoods thickened into a dense break near the stream and spread out over the hills. They were silent men, stern and forbidding, for they were bound on a mission of death. One of them rode with head bowed forward on his breast. A thin trickle of blood had dried on his cheek. His boots were looped together underneath the horse, and his hands were lashed behind him. A grim-faced cowboy led the horse.

"I tell you, you're hangin' the wrong

man!" the prisoner cried out passionately. "I didn't kill him! I never killed anyone. I don't know anything about it."

"Yeah?" drawled big Tom Train of the Double Q spread. "Don't lie, you skunk. Cal Steele seen you shoot him in the back while he was brandin' calves. Bud was one of our boys, an' we don't allow nobody to dry-gulch our waddies. No, sir!"

"Cal Steele is a dirty liar!" shouted the prisoner. "I didn't. . . ."

"Shut up!"

A man riding a beautiful roan gelding whirled upon him and struck him in the face with his hand. "Call me a dirty liar, will you, Jim Hankins?" he gritted, his hands clenching and his face red with rage.

"Yes, you're a dirty liar," Jim retorted defiantly.

"Damn you, I'll. . . ."

The calm voice of Tom Train brought Cal up sharp. "What the hell, Cal, did you expect him to own up an' say he done it?"

Cal Steele hesitated, then rode on, his face pale after his hot anger. He was young, not more than twenty-two, and dressed with a meticulous care that was in sharp contrast to the weather-worn outfits of the other men. His hat was a soft, gray Stetson. Instead of the usual neckerchief, he wore a

48

black bow tie in the collar of his blue silk shirt. A doeskin vest of soft tan was elaborate with fancy stitching. A pearl-handled .45 swung at his side, and his saddle was ornate with silver mountings and stamped leather. His batwing chaps were white, contrasting strangely with the bull-leather and rough-hair leg coverings of the other men. A range dude. The name, however, was applied only when Cal's back was turned, for he was a bad *hombre* with a gun, and his quick, violent temper made him doubly dangerous. He had inherited the Slash M Ranch, but it was rumored that he had lost so much money to Lute Hodnette, banker, saloon keeper, gambler, and owner of most of Buffalo Gap, that Lute really owned the ranch and Cal was working for him. Lately he had spent much of his time at the Bar T Bar spread, the attraction being Ellen Vale, the fair owner.

As the five men approached the fringe of trees, Jim Hankins continued his appeal. "Anyway," he protested at last, "I've got a right to a fair trial."

"That's where you're wrong," growled Brad Wheatley. "A nester ain't got no right to a trial or anything else."

"I know that's the way you figure," Jim answered quietly. "If you're hangin' me 'cause

I'm a farmer, then I ain't got nothin' to say. If you're hangin' me for shootin' Bud Kelley, you're hangin' the wrong man."

There was no answer. The men pulled up under a cottonwood tree with a convenient limb. One of them threw his rope over it and adjusted the noose around the prisoner's neck.

A rapid drumming of hoofs sounded from the prairie, and a small pinto burst into the grove. Riding it was a wide-eyed girl, wearing a fringed riding skirt, a white shirt-waist, and a broad-brimmed Stetson hat.

"I knew it!" she cried, her eyes blazing. "You sha'n't hang him." Defiantly she faced the little group. "You . . . you cowards!"

"Now looky here, Miss Vale," Tom Train began. "You're hornin' in where it ain't none o' your affair. Or leastways, you should stick with your friends instead o' your enemies. This here is the nester that shot Bud Kelley in the back."

"You lie!" cried Jim Hankins. "I didn't even know he was dead till you fellows told me."

"Cal Steele seen him," Tom continued without heeding the interruption. "You know how it is, Miss Vale. A killer has to be strung up . . . *pronto*. It's the only way when you ain't got no more law courts than we have in this country."

"You sha'n't hang him!" the girl repeated. She drew up to the condemned man and reached for the noose around his neck.

With an oath Cal Steele dashed forward, seized the bridle of the pinto, and dragged it forward. "Go ahead!" he ordered viciously. "Drive that horse out from under him!"

With blazing eyes the girl struck at him with her quirt, then sprang to the ground. In a moment Cal was off his horse and had seized her in a paralyzing grip. "You're buttin' into somethin' that is none of your business, Ellen," he told her through drawn lips. Then he called to the others: "Go ahead an' hang him. If she don't like to see it, she kin turn the other way."

Chivalry was strong in those men, but Hank Trellis and Brad Wheatley moved forward at Cal's command. Hank pulled the rope taut and tied it to the trunk of the tree. Brad seized the bridle and urged the horse forward.

Again the girl screamed, and struggled to free herself from Cal's arms.

"Git it over with!" Cal cried. "His friends know we've got him, an' they may be here any minute."

The horse started. With a choking cry Jim Hankins swung into space.

Ellen moaned and hid her eyes.

The sharp crack of a gun echoed through the grove. A strand of the rope gave way and began unwinding. Again the gun roared. The rope parted, and Jim Hankins fell heavily to the ground.

Ellen looked up as Cal released her and lifted his hands. The others also were standing with hands raised. A short distance away, motionless as a statue, was a man on a gray horse. A long, gray cloak was thrown over his shoulders. A gray hat was on his head, and a gray mask over his eyes.

Ellen broke the sharp silence. "The gray rider," she murmured, awe in her voice.

II

"A Promise"

Ellen had heard many tales of terror about this man of mystery who, they said, swooped down upon isolated ranches or farms, killing, robbing, torturing, destroying. No one had ever seen him except alone, yet such was his uncanny skill with a gun, so quick was he in movement and action, and so swift was his gray horse, that his face had never been seen, and strong men had been unable to bring him to justice. It had been the general belief that he had perished in Crazy Horse River five years ago, with a posse close upon his heels. Yet here he was today, and Ellen realized that the rumors of his return were true, and that this was not the first time that he had reappeared in his new rôle of a protector of nesters rather than as a scourge to both farmers and cattlemen.

The silence of the grave had fallen in the little grove. The sun was long down, and the gray rider seemed ghostly and indistinct in the twilight. No one spoke or moved — a grim testimonial to the dread of the gray rider, for these were men who did not hesitate to take a chance.

Ellen felt a movement at her side. Cal Steele was stealthily drawing his gun. As it leaped from his holster, the weapon of the gray rider roared. Cal's half-drawn iron fell to the ground, and he clutched a numb and tingling hand.

"Don't try that again," came a clear, calm drawl, "or it'll be the heart next time, instead of the hand." There was a dead silence, and then the voice went on: "There ain't goin' to be no hangin'." To Jim Hankins he said: "Git up there, you, *hombre* on the ground, an' make yourself scarce."

Hankins sat up and removed the noose from his neck. He looked nervously at his would-be executioners, scrambled into his saddle, and then rode quickly out of the grove.

Then the slow drawl of the gray rider came again: "I'm backin' away now, an' probably some of you will want to try a shot at me. God help you if you do."

Keeping his gun trained on the five men, he backed the gray for a few yards and then turned deliberately and disappeared among the trees.

Tom Train began to swear softly. Then he shot a sharp glance at Ellen. "I beg your pardon, Miss Vale," he apologized, "but I plumb forgot. What the hell, anyway? Here are five danged cowpokes with shootin' irons, an' we ain't even got the spunk to hang a dry-gulchin' nester. Of all the yella. . . ."

"He had the drop on us," Hank interposed lamely. "You seen what he done to Cal."

Cal turned to Ellen with a forced smile. "I want to apologize for the way I treated you, Ellen, but you see how it is. We got to fight or quit ranchin'. There ain't room for both us an' the nesters. We got the cattle. They got the water. One of us has got to go."

Ellen turned her back without speaking and went to her horse. Angrily he followed.

"Well!" he snapped. "I apologized, an' I'm waitin' for an answer."

Coolly she turned toward him, looked at him a moment, and then mounted the pinto. "You have done exactly what I would expect of you," she told him calmly, as she started toward the trail.

"Ellen!" He followed along by her side. "Ellen, you know how I feel about you an'...."

"I know," she interrupted. "Please don't tell me again. It will only make me repeat what I have said before. If you were the only man in the world, I wouldn't marry you."

His face flamed, and he drew back. He started to retort.

A gun barked. A bullet zipped past, struck a limb, and went whining away in the twilight. Through the trees a dozen riders had come close, indistinct in the fast-deepening gloom. The cowboys dropped flat on the ground.

"What the hell do you want?" shouted Tom Train.

"We want you damn' cattlemen!" They recognized the voice of Jim Hankins.

Bullets crashed about them, and sharp stabs of flame appeared among the trees.

The cowboys answered the fire, Cal shouting from behind Ellen's horse.

Ellen urged the pinto forward. It leaped at the touch of the spur, then reared high with a shrill scream, and pitched to the ground. It rose partly to its hoofs, then sank back. Quick as its movement had been, Ellen, too, was quick enough to draw her foot from the stirrup.

The nesters were pouring out their hot lead, and Ellen knew they could not recognize her as a woman in the darkness. The vicious snarl of bullets sounded on every side. The cowboys had crept behind the trees.

Brad Wheatley cried out in a strangling voice, pitched forward, and lay still.

Ellen leaped to her feet and ran between the trees. A bullet sang by, dangerously close, and she had the fleeting thought that one of the cowboys had fired at her by mistake. There was a drumming of hoofs behind her, and suddenly she felt herself lifted from the ground. A man had swept her up and was holding her before him on the saddle.

III

"Ellen Makes a Promise"

Behind sounded the cracking of guns. The horse zigzagged swiftly between the trees, dodging like an antelope.

"The gray rider!" a voice shouted, and Ellen recognized the voice of Cal Steele. "The gray rider got Ellen! Kill him! Stop shootin' at us, you damn' nesters, an' help me rescue the girl."

The sharp *zip* of bullets whipped past them. But the gray rider was carefully shielding the girl's body with his own. Close to Ellen's face was his gray mask. He was holding her tightly against him, and she realized that she was completely in the power of the man who had terrorized the district. If the tales about him were true. . . .

She screamed once, and then the world grew suddenly black. As she struggled back to consciousness, she could still hear the sound of guns. The gray rider was speaking, and she listened without attempting to struggle or scream.

"I wouldn't hurt a hair of your head, miss," he was saying. "I saw the fight you was puttin' up for the nester, an' I come in to back your play. Them nesters is all loco an' would 'a' killed you, prob'ly, if I hadn't come back. They didn't even know you was a girl. I'm takin' you straight home, miss, jest as soon as we shake off this bunch that's followin'. I don't know if it's the cow waddies, nesters, or both."

She saw they were making directly toward the cottonwood break near the stream. The saplings were quite thick for a mile or more, but the gray horse never paused. Straight into the thicket he dashed — dodging, twisting, turning. Like a jack rabbit. The branches lashed his riders as they swept past. A sharp turn to the right and the shouting grew farther away.

For a mile or so they kept on through the thicket. Then another turn brought them out on the prairie. Far behind they could hear sounds of pursuit, and presently the shooting was resumed.

The gray rider chuckled. "Them *hombres* are at it again," he drawled. "I guess all of 'em come after us, but a nester an' a cow-poke can't keep out of a fight very long. Now, miss, tell me where you live, an' we'll go there *pronto* if not sooner."

"Straight ahead to the trail," she told him, "and then turn to the right. The ranch is not more than four miles."

For some time they rode on in silence. Then Ellen realized suddenly that he was still holding her close. Gently she disengaged herself.

"I . . . I can ride now," she said.

He slipped behind the saddle, and she put her feet in the stirrups.

Not another word was spoken till they topped a sharp rise and saw the lights of the Bar T Bar gleaming before them. Ellen was proud of the spread. She had kept it as her father had left it when he died. A huge ranch house like a Spanish *hacienda* was surrounded by a green lawn dotted with trees. Behind were the spacious corrals and a dozen other buildings.

They pulled up at the front gate, and Ellen slipped from the saddle. Wonderingly she looked into the eyes that reflected back the light through holes in the mask.

"I . . . I don't know how to thank you . . . ," she began.

"Please don't try." He lifted his hat ever so slightly and bowed. "It's shore been a pleasure, miss. A pleasure I wouldn't 'a' missed."

Slowly he turned the horse's head and

started away. Impulsively Ellen took a step toward him.

"But can't I do something in return?" she asked. "I . . . I don't like to be under obligations."

He stopped and faced her. "Yes, you can do something, miss," he drawled. "Jest don't believe all the mean stories you hear about the gray rider. That'll make me feel plumb good."

"You . . . you mean the stories they tell of you are not true?"

"Yeah, most of 'em ain't true."

"I will believe you," she assured him. "Especially after what you have done tonight."

She stood, watching, as he disappeared in the darkness.

IV

"The Professor"

Four cursing men rode toward the Circle D, a small ranch, lightly stocked, owned by a young newcomer, Mel Bryant. Two of them were bleeding from wounds, and the body of Brad Wheatley was tied to the horse that had belonged to the dead cowboy.

"Bryant has got two men besides that crazy professor that's always moonin' around on the flats," remarked Tom Train, who had a flesh wound in the left side. "We'll git patched up an' then hit the trail after that damned gray rider."

"Go after him all you want." Cal Steele yanked his horse viciously, for he was in an ugly mood. "I'm hittin' the trail for Buffalo Gap."

Tom stared at him. "You don't mean you ain't goin' after him? Why, folks say Ellen is a sort of a cousin of yourn, an' everybody knows you been tryin' to marry her."

"Everybody knows too damned much," Cal retorted. "If she had minded her own business, we'd have hung that nester an' been on our way long before the rest o' the crowd come up." He glowered at the men. "And that ain't all. This Bryant *hombre* that's bought the Circle D ain't salty none whatever. He won't take sides with us, an' I don't reckon his men will. They ain't worth a cuss, anyway. I wish my own waddies had been with me today. *There's* some men that kin shoot as well as stuff beans down their necks."

"What's all this talk about the crazy professor?" asked Hank Trellis, who was in no mood for a quarrel. "He's buildin' some kind of a tower over on the flats with a big wheel on top of it. Zeno Wiggins asked him what it was for, an' he said it was to make it rain. Zeno 'bout died a-laughin'. The danged fool ought to know you can't make it rain in this country. He's shore crazy."

"Yeah," Tom put in, "I've hear 'n' tell he's coo-coo. But Mel Bryant is all right. He looks like a good *hombre* an' acts like one."

"All right like a buzzard," Cal snapped. "If he was all right, he'd join with the cattlemen against these damned nesters. It's his fight as well as ours. He's only got two little water holes on the whole place. When they dry up, he's through." Without another word, he turned into a trail that forked away toward Buffalo Gap.

"Let the skunk go," murmured Tom in a low voice. "He hid behind the gal's horse an' then behind a tree all durin' the fight. He's yella."

They did not see a rider pass some distance ahead of them, and then turn from the trail and ride after Cal. Presently they drew up before the rambling house of the Circle D. The door opened at their hail, and a tall, stooped, bespectacled man stood framed in the doorway.

"Where's Mel?" Tom asked.

"Buffalo Gap," was the answer. "He probably will not return till quite late. But come in, gentlemen. I see you have been in trouble."

They carried the body of Brad Wheatley into the room, covered it with a blanket, and then stripped to present their injuries. The professor brought hot water and bandages, and proved himself to be an adept at dressing wounds.

"Now," he said, "there are spare beds here and two or three bunks in the house where the men sleep. Make yourselves at home, gentlemen. You need the rest and quiet."

"Not us," growled Tom Train. "We gotta be on the move. We're headin' for the Bar T Bar."

Briefly he told of Ellen Vale and the gray rider.

"You need not worry, gentlemen," the professor informed them when Tom concluded. "Miss Vale reached home safely."

"How do you know?" Tom asked.

The professor made a deprecating gesture with his long arms and smiled. "I know many things, my friends, but I seldom give the source of my information. To do so would injure my reputation for wisdom."

"Well, we're headin' for the Bar T Bar."

Tom stalked from the room with the

others following. Arriving shortly after at the Vale Ranch, they roused nine sleepy men from the bunkhouse.

"What the hell you talkin' 'bout?" Lance Craig, the foreman, asked as Tom concluded his story. "Ellen come in right after dark, an' left in the buckboard to meet a school friend in Buffalo Gap. She never said nothin' about a fight with nesters or a gray rider. You *hombres* must have been on one hell of a spree."

"Well, what do you know?" Hank Trellis scratched his head and looked at Tom. "That danged professor gives me the creeps."

"Yeah," Tom said, remembering. "He must be some kind of magician."

"Jest the same," Hank went on stubbornly, "I'm layin' two to one he can't make it rain."

In Buffalo Gap, Cal Steele threw the reins of his tired, blowing mount over a hitch rack and strode through the swing doors of The Ranchers' Rest, saloon and dance-hall headquarters of Lute Hodnette. There was a pleased little cry, and a dance-hall girl, ornate with rouge and cheap jewelry, ran to Cal with outstretched arms.

"Honey, honey," she cooed as she threw

her arms about his neck.

Roughly he pushed her from him. "Git away!" he snapped.

Wondering, she followed him to the bar. "What's the matter, honey?" she asked in a hurt tone. "Don't you love me any more?"

"Git out!" he snarled.

Seizing a bottle that stood at the bar, he poured a stiff peg and drank it at a gulp.

"Where's Hod?" he asked the bartender.

"In the office."

Without a word or a glance at the girl, he strode to a door behind the bar and entered a large, well-furnished room. A heavy man, squat, powerful, with a bulbous nose and small eyes, was seated at a table, figuring. A bottle and several glasses were before him. He looked up and grunted as Cal sank into a chair.

"Well?" he asked after a pause, "what's the boy been doing? Any more mischief?"

"Haven't you heard?"

"No."

Cal poured a drink from the bottle, and studied the expressionless face before him. "I told you, Hodnette, that you would never have the chance of foreclosin' the Slash M."

The big man sank back in the chair and folded his hands over his paunch.

"I told you," Cal went on, "that I was

goin' to be head man on this range."

Hodnette grunted, and the cowboy poured another drink.

"A month ago a nester was found dead by his cabin. A few days later Slim Hargreaves of the Bar S was killed while ridin' fence. Last week another nester was killed."

"Yes," grunted Hodnette, "I know. You killed 'em to stir up trouble between nesters and ranchers."

Cal gulped his drink. "Mebbe so. This is a dry year. If I don't git into Spring River Valley, I'll lose what cattle I got left. If this fight goes far enough, the nesters'll leave, an' I'll git what I want. I told you I was goin' to."

"Well?" asked Hodnette after a pause.

"Today Bud Kelley of the Double Q was shot by a water hole."

"Shot in the back?" the other asked.

"What difference does it make where he was shot?"

"Well?"

"Well, I'm afraid I . . . that is, the man that shot Bud Kelley . . . was seen when he rode away."

"Who by?"

"Mel Bryant."

"The one that's puttin' up the rain-makin' machine?"

"Yeah. I'm not shore he saw me, but he come over the hill jest afterwards, an' I saw *him*."

Hodnette pursed his thick lips and frowned. "Why didn't you gun him?" he asked.

" 'Cause Tom Train and his boys were jest over the hill, an' I was afraid they heard the shot. I went direct to 'em with a story that Jim Hankins done it. I couldn't take chances on 'em comin' over the hill an' seein' me gun Mel Bryant. Jim Hankins was home, an' we rounded him up and were to make cotton-wood fruit outta him."

"Did you?"

Cal poured the glass half full of whisky and drank it slowly. "About fifteen nesters come a little too soon, an' we had to leave," he explained thickly.

For some time Hodnette regarded the dashing cowboy with unblinking eyes. "Cal," he said at last, "you would be a good man for me, only you're yella. You know my game. I'm after most of this range. I don't git in bad with the law because I let others do the work. That's where you come in."

Cal swore under his breath, and again reached for the bottle.

"No more of that!" Hodnette spoke in a sharp voice. "I say you're yella, but I'm playin' with you because you're the best I kin get. I'm after this range."

"All except my spread and the Bar T Bar," Cal stated thickly.

"Yeah, I'll leave you your ranch, and I can't git the Bar T Bar. It has water, hay, and range. It's always been a moneymaker and is out of debt. I can't git Ellen Vale in a poker game the way I did you. So I'm not after her ranch."

"Well, I am." Cal looked up defiantly. "I'm workin' my place an' gittin' the Bar T Bar."

"How? She won't marry you."

"No, damn her! But I'm her fourth cousin an' nearest relation."

"Meanin' what?"

"If she dies, I git everything."

Hodnette looked at the drunken cowboy with his small, expressionless eyes. "You ain't got the nerve to do it," he said finally.

"The hell I ain't! I say I'm goin' to be the big shot on this range!"

"As a matter of fact," Hodnette went on quietly, "you're not her cousin a-tall. Bill Steele found you when you was a little shaver and never legally 'dopted you. But nobody knows that but me, and I'm not workin'. A few years ago I had a real man workin' for me. Nobody knew who he was,

68

but he done for plenty people that got in my way. He went masked, and dressed all in gray."

Cal sat up and stared at the man before him. "The gray rider!" he exclaimed.

"Well?"

"What become of him?" The thickness was gone from Cal's speech.

"He got drowned in the Crazy Horse River."

"He's been seen three times this last week," Cal stated quietly. "He busted in three times when we was about to git a nester. He's stickin' up for 'em against the cattlemen. He held us all up today an' turned Jim Hankins loose. Shot the rope in two as Jim was swingin'."

Hodnette sat silent for some time. "You had too much red-eye, Cal," he stated finally. "I know the gray rider died five years ago. I pulled him out of the river and buried him myself."

"Well, I shore saw the gray rider today."

Hodnette shuddered in spite of himself. The gray rider! It would certainly be bad for him if that ghostly terror could return, for Hodnette himself had set the trap that brought about the death of his minion. The gray rider knew too much about Lute Hodnette. He peered out of the open window into the darkness. With an effort he smiled. Why should he fear? The gray rider was dead all right. "Ellen Vale is in town," he said presently. "She drove a buckboard in about an hour ago. Come in alone."

Cal sprang to his feet.

"Alone!" he cried. "Say!" He paused thoughtfully. "My boys ought to be in by now. I'll. . . ."

He stopped, and strode from the room.

Hodnette chuckled and poured himself a drink. Neither of them had seen a face peep quickly in at the window and then disappear into the night.

V

"To Tomorrow"

Hodnette worked at his figures for some time, and then contemplated them with a sigh. It was an imposing total set before him, the accumulation of years of gambling and crime. Yet it probably was not entirely the desire for money that drove Lute Hodnette forward in his life. Nor was it thirst for power. His was the nature of a great, hairy spider that lies concealed in its den, gradually capturing the insect life about it — silent, impassive, emotionless, deadly, hiding, laboring, planning, destroying, until only the spider remains.

Cal Steele was one of his best tools, but he was only one of the little spiders that bring the flies to the net of the great one. Tomorrow would bring the culmination of years of effort — a pitched battle between the nesters and cowboys. Cal and Lute's other hirelings knew this, but they did not know that the nesters would be reinforced by a dozen hired guns. Suspecting an easy victory with the ranchers, Hodnette was planning for his own men, along with the others, to be destroyed.

Hodnette had planned carefully, had worked silently. He had brought in the nesters and financed them, thus shutting off the water from the cattle — water, of not much importance ordinarily, but vital in a dry year.

Hodnette had staked the nesters. He had lent money to the ranchers. He dealt in small amounts, it is true, for his capital had to be spread out very thin. But a small mortgage became a great one when owners were at war, when men died overnight, and there was no one left to bid on land and cattle that were offered for sale under the sheriff's hammer.

Tomorrow!

The ranchers must have the priceless water. The nesters were defending their homes. Murder had been done. Feeling was at a pitch where men asked only to kill. Tomorrow the two forces would meet on the flats near the tower the crazy professor had built to bring rain, where there was no shelter for fighting men.

With a smile on his thick lips, Lute Hodnette lifted his gaze. "Tomorrow," he murmured, and drank the fiery liquid.

He was aroused from his reverie by a soft step behind him.

"Well?" he asked without turning. Lute Hodnette feared no man.

There came the sound of the heavy curtain being drawn over the window, and then Hodnette turned, faced a somber specter.

For a long time he stared at the apparition that confronted him, his eyes wide, his lips parted. He was dimly conscious of the round orifice in a gun held in a steady hand.

"Serge Bassett," he whispered.

The other remained silent, his gray cloak wrapped around him, gray mask over his eyes.

"You . . . you wasn't dead?" The whispered words were scarcely audible.

"Do the dead stay in their graves, or do they come back to haunt us?"

A rush of blood came suddenly back to Hodnette's pasty face. "What do you want?"

"Lute Hodnette!" The voice came, low and tense, from between tightly compressed lips. "You've got one chance to leave this room alive. Take your pen and write the story of what you've done, the story of the gray rider, the story of Cal Steele, the story of your crimes."

For a long moment Lute stared into the eyes that burned through the holes in the gray mask. "My God!" he groaned. "Not that!"

Slowly the gun barrel approached. It drew near to his forehead and touched him.

With a low cry he turned, seized the pen, and began to write feverishly, the fear of death upon him. His face and neck were red with congealed blood. Perspiration dripped from his brow. Page by page the story was written.

The gray rider, staring over Hodnette's shoulder, read as the saloon man wrote. He started slightly as Hodnette told of the coming battle that was to take place on the baked flats near the rainmaker's tower to-morrow.

"Now, sign," he ordered as the story was concluded.

Hodnette passed his hand over his brow. Then he scrawled his name in big letters. The signature ended in a splatter, and the pen fell from nerveless fingers.

"God!" he gasped. "The light."

With a strangling cry he fell forward across the table. His hand, flung out, scattered the papers before him. His hoarse breathing ceased, and he lay still.

Lute Hodnette had died from his warring emotions, and arteries that were rotten from the way he'd lived.

Ellen Vale had driven to town to meet a school friend, Dot Lacey, who would come on the late stage. She left her team at the livery barn, and then looked at her watch. She was very tired.

"Four hours to wait," she murmured.

Going to the hotel, she engaged a room on the ground floor. She determined to lie down and wait there, and then both girls could stay in town until morning.

Leaving a request that she be called in time for the stage, she went down the dim hall, into the room, and threw herself on the bed fully dressed. In a moment she was asleep.

She was awakened by a tapping at the door.

"Time for the stage?" she called in a sleepy voice.

Again the tapping came. Arising hastily, she went to the door and threw it open. Cal Steele loomed before her. And the next instant a blanket was thrown over her head, stifling her scream. Strong hands seized her. Half choked, gasping for breath, she knew that she was carried for some distance and thrown across a saddle. Followed the rough motion of a trotting horse and presently the blanket was removed. Several men were grouped about her. She fought anger and fear as she tried to still the wild beating of her heart.

Her bonds were cut, and she was lifted down. A full moon was high, and by its light she recognized the buildings of the Slash M, Cal Steele's ranch.

A huge red-bearded man lifted her and carried her into the house where he lighted a lamp. She heard Cal's voice as he directed his men.

"You gotta git some sleep now. There'll be hot work tomorrow. Mort'll keep watch."

He entered the room and motioned to the red-bearded giant to withdraw.

"Watch the house," he ordered in a low

voice. "Nobody saw us git her out of the hotel, but it pays to be careful."

Standing close against the wall, Ellen watched Cal pour a drink from a bottle on the table and toss it off. Then he looked at her directly for the first time.

"It's a showdown, Ellen," he announced thickly, and she saw that he was dangerously drunk. "I'm the head man . . . the head man of this range. Nothin' kin stop me. Hodnette thinks he's got me hawg-tied, but I'll show him!"

Silently she listened, a sick fear in her heart, at his thick speech and the strange glitter in his eyes.

"I'm the head man," he repeated. "Tomorrow the nesters git cleaned out. I'll grab a big slice of hay land. I'll show Hodnette, but I gotta have the Bar T Bar to do it."

He poured out another drink and gulped it down.

"You hear me, Ellen," he went on. "I gotta have the Bar T Bar. It'll give me all I need. When I've got him where I want him, I'll kill him. I'll be a king, Ellen, an' you kin be my queen."

Calmly Ellen faced him. "Stop this play-acting, Cal. You know I'll never marry you. You call yourself the head man, but others call you a silly range dude. You'll never get the Bar T Bar by marrying me."

"Then there's only one way to it, I reckon." Cal faced Ellen with blazing eyes. "You forgit, young lady, that I'm your nearest relation. Tomorrow you'll be found on a horse at the bottom of the red cliffs. Nobody will know how you got there, but I'll weep at your funeral an' walk into the Bar T Bar."

Ellen shrank against the wall, a numb terror gripping her heart. "You . . . you wouldn't dare."

"Oh, wouldn't I?" He shrugged. "You got your choice, an' I don't give a damn which it is. I know a dozen girls I'd rather marry, but I'll do the fair thing. We'll go tonight to Wimbleton an' git married, or . . . you'll go over the red cliffs. Take your choice."

"I never will marry you, Cal," Ellen said coldly. "And I am not afraid to die."

Silently he regarded her with flaming, bloodshot eyes. Then his laugh was hard, brutal, as he started toward her.

VI

"Five Miles to Go"

A man rode out of the moonlight and went straight to the Slash M buildings. A gray cloak was wrapped about him, and a gray mask covered his eyes. He stopped in the deep shadow of the house, dismounted quietly, and slipped around to the front porch. A huge man was bent over, close to the door, evidently listening at the keyhole. He rose with a jerk as the gray form approached. The barrel of a .45 struck him just over the temple, and he went down without a cry.

Softly the gray rider turned the doorknob and entered the room. For a few moments he stood motionless, with arms folded across his breast. In the room was Ellen Vale, white and calm, and her large eyes were upon him. Cal Steele was creeping toward her. As though some sixth sense warned him, he turned. His red eyes opened wide; his jaw dropped. Slowly he raised his hands.

"I didn't say to stick 'em up," a slow voice

drawled. "I'm givin' you a chance to go for your gun. Folks say you're greased lightnin' on the draw. Let's see what you got in the way of speed."

Like a trapped rabbit, Cal looked at the masked face before him. His trembling hands came down, and he swallowed hard. Death, he knew, was very near.

"My . . . my gun," he mumbled. "It . . . it ain't loaded. Cartridges . . . here . . . in the drawer. . . ."

He took a step toward the table. The gray rider watched him without moving. Then Cal sprang. His hand crashed down. The lamp flew into a thousand pieces against the wall, and the room was in total darkness.

There came the sound of a door opening and slamming shut, and a laugh floated through the house. It was not a laugh of mirth. It was the cackle of a man who had looked death in the face and cheated it.

A moment later another door closed, and Cal's shout rang out from the outside, yelling to his men.

The gray rider opened the door, letting in a flood of moonlight. "Quick, Ellen . . . Miss Vale! This way!"

Ellen sprang to his side and seized his outstretched hand. Cal was halfway to the bunkhouse as they dashed outside.

"The gray rider!" Cal was yelling. "Git him! He's alone. Quick, you sons, an' come a-shootin'!"

Holding Ellen by the hand, the gray rider dashed around the house.

"Take my hoss, Miss Vale!" he commanded. "I'll hold 'em here till you git away."

"I will not! You sha'n't stay here to die!"

"It's the best way," he told her hurriedly. "We can't beat 'em ridin' double."

"Then I'll stay here with you."

Ellen's voice was final, and he growled something under his breath. They could hear Cal urging his men forward.

"Will you come?" Ellen asked, her voice determined.

With a quick motion the gray rider seized her, lifted her into the saddle, and sprang up behind. Digging the gray horse forward, they rode out into the moonlight.

"There they go!" Cal shouted. "We'll run 'em down easy on the prairie!"

The gray horse stretched into a swift stride in spite of his double burden. He was capable of continuing at that speed until his great heart stopped beating. The gray rider slipped a rifle from its sheath and threw a cartridge into the chamber.

"Speed can't win us out of this," he muttered. "We gotta fool 'em if we kin."

Ellen guided the horse.

"To the left," he told her. "There are some good hills ahead, and there is a lot of brush along a dry creek."

They had covered less than two miles when three black dots appeared behind them, and then two more. Steadily these spots grew larger. Cal was making every effort to catch them while they were still on his range. Twice the gray rider turned and fired, although there was not the slightest chance of hitting anyone at that distance.

"Just to let 'em know I got a rifle," he said quietly. "If they're dependin' on six-shooters, we might show 'em somethin' yet."

The gray cloak impeded his movement, and he loosed it from his shoulders and let it fall. Then he tore the mask from his face.

"Why, Mel Bryant!" she exclaimed.

He grinned. "You see, Miss Ellen" — he was talking jerkily as they sped on — "I knew there was somethin' funny about this mess. I happened to see a couple of cowboys after a nester one day, an' I stopped the killin' by puttin' on this mask and cloak that I wore in a play in school. I didn't know then that a gray rider had a reputation in this country before. Three times I helped a nester, an' the old cloak come in mighty handy 'cause it scared the daylights out of 'em. I couldn't let 'em know it was me, because I was fightin' against my own people, the ranchers. Then I heard about the real gray rider that everybody was after. I suddenly found everybody against me. I heard something tonight that changed the whole thing. Then I found out you'd been carried off, an' I knew Cal had you."

"How did you know?" she asked.

"I heard him talking with Hodnette. Then a girl came on the stage an' asked for you. They tried to call you in the hotel an' found you were gone. I knew Cal was at the bottom of it on account of what I heard him say to Hodnette."

There came a sharp sound of a bullet as it snarled nearby.

"One of 'em has a rifle," Mel commented tersely. "Make for that hill an' go straight over it."

The gray horse was blowing and dripping with sweat as they topped the hill. Mel sprang to the ground, and threw himself flat.

"Go on down out of sight," he ordered. "They'll think we're makin' a stand, an' it'll mebbe delay 'em. Or, better yet, go on alone an' let me hold 'em here."

"You know I will not!" she retorted indignantly.

He fired twice at the three men who came within range. They paused and waited for the others. Shooting once more, Mel jerked the empty shell from the gun and stuffed cartridges into the magazine as he ran to where Ellen awaited him.

"Quick! Around that hill to the south!" he cried.

Just as they reached it, a shout came from behind. Their pursuers charged directly toward them. With the moon turning night into day, there seemed little chance of escaping. As they rounded the hill, Ellen could see the thin, black line of the brush lying a mile or two ahead. It stretched along a dry creekbed a mile or more and was two or three hundred yards wide.

"We'll try straight for it on a dead run," Mel said. "If we kin make it, mebbe we can stand 'em off till Dick is rested. Come on, boy!"

Nobly the animal responded to his shout and the touch of the spur. A bullet sang past, and then another. Mel turned and fired.

Closer the pursuers came. The gray horse was straining to the utmost. His nostrils were distended. Lather covered his sides, and his flanks heaved.

Straight into the brush they rode, and Mel jumped from the saddle. He was firing as he reached the ground, and the men, scarcely a hundred yards away, halted sharply.

"Go 'round on the other side, Buck an' Wilson!" Cal's order came to them distinctly, and two men made a wide detour to the other side of the brush.

"Better lie down flat," Mel cautioned. "They'll be rakin' the brush with bullets in a minute. As soon as Dick has had a chance to blow, we'll ride straight down the creek."

Ellen came to his side.

"Give me your revolver, Mel." Her voice was courageous, and she smiled. He handed her the gun.

The five men on the prairie were lying down and raking the brush with their gunfire. But they were too far away for accurate shooting.

"I might git a hoss, if they come a little closer," Mel said. "But, Lordy, how I hate to shoot a hoss!"

"Close in over there!" Cal called to the men on the other side of the thicket. "He can't watch both sides."

"Keep shooting," Mel whispered to Ellen.

He dashed across the thicket, and a moment later his rifle roared again and again.

It seemed to Ellen that the men on the

84

prairie were creeping nearer. She fired till the gun barrel was hot, and then waited silently. A half hour or more passed as Mel and their besiegers exchanged intermittent shots, and then Mel was at her side.

"Come." He reached out a hand and helped her to her feet. "Dick is all right now. We'll try again."

They mounted hastily and turned down the dry creek that often was a raging torrent in the spring. Its sand bed was dry and hard. Straight along it they dashed, and a few minutes later came out a mile below at the other end of the thicket.

They headed into the east where there was a faint streak of gray. It would not be long till dawn.

A shout sounded behind them.

"They've seen us!" Mel said quietly. "It's nip and tuck now . . . with five miles to go."

VII

"The Rainmaker"

The ride over those five last miles remained in Ellen's consciousness like a dream.

Straight ahead she guided the gray horse that was straining to the last ounce of his strength with the double load. Time after time Mel turned and fired at the men who pressed closer and closer. Bullet after bullet whipped past them. Finally Mel stopped shooting.

"Three cartridges left," he told Ellen. "I'll have to save 'em for a last stand. I sure wish you had gone on and left me at Cal's ranch."

It seemed hours later before he spoke again.

"A little to the left. You can see the tower if you look sharp."

Presently she caught sight of it, a high, boarded structure with some kind of a huge, wheel-shaped device at the top. She had heard the boys call it the crazy professor's rainmaker.

Mel fired once more as they reached it. Then he was off the horse and dragged her from the saddle. The pursuers were close behind. A bullet fanned Mel's cheek as he hurried Ellen through the open door of the tower. His arm jerked, and he slipped to his knees.

"Flat on the floor," he mumbled, his voice thick. "Bullets'll go through these boards like they were paper."

He blazed away through the cracks with his handgun.

"They've got us surrounded," he told her presently. "They'll rake the place from every side. It's goin' to be a close shave . . . if I can keep 'em far enough away. But every one of 'em has a rifle, an' they must have plenty of shells."

The steady crack of the rifles came from all sides. Bullets ripped through the frail shelter, snarling above them, tearing splinters from the boards that stung as they touched hands and faces.

Slowly the gray widened in the east, and slowly it turned to red, and then to gold. Mel could see Ellen's face now, and she smiled at him bravely. Then her expression changed as she saw his left arm hanging limply at his side.

"Mel!" she cried. "You're hurt!"

"Jest a scratch," he assured her. "They got me jest as I come through the door."

Once they heard Cal Steele's voice.

"Dash in an' git 'em, you damned cowards!" he cried.

"Go in an' git 'em yourself," answered a voice from the other side of the tower. "That *hombre* kin shoot."

Slowly the sun poked its golden rim above the horizon and sent a flood of light over the burned prairie.

"Mel!" Ellen cried suddenly. "I see men

off there a couple of miles. There must be fifty or more."

"Yeah," he answered weakly. "They will be comin' from the other direction, too. The nesters an' ranchers are bein' steered straight into each other so they kin wipe each other out. It was part of Lute Hodnette's scheme."

He sank down and groaned.

"Ellen," he pleaded a moment later, "kin you cut up my shirt an' bind my arm to my side?"

"Mel, you are hurt badly," she cried.

"Arm's busted above the elbow, an' it flops when I move. Here's my knife."

With tight lips she cut strips from his shirt, tied them together in a long bandage, put a compress over an ugly wound in the arm, and bound it to his body. It was not the first time Ellen had dressed wounds.

"I gotta go up there on the ladder," he told her as he nodded to the top of the tower.

"Mel, they'll kill you!"

The bullets were smashing through the thin boards as though the men had decided to end it in a single burst of gunfire. The body of men in the south drew closer.

"I've got to do it," Mel declared as he struggled to his feet. "It's the only way to stop a pitched battle between 'em. Professor Hendricks has it all ready."

"Professor Hendricks! Is he the one everybody says is crazy?"

Mel smiled. "He knows more than all of us put together. He's out here for his health and showed me the way to save the country. The whole range is underlaid with a sort of lake that reached two or three hundred miles from the mountains. He's traveled in Holland and knows how to bring water by deep drillin'. Don't watch, Ellen. Lie flat and they can't hit you."

"Mel!"

Again he smiled and held out his hand. Impulsively she leaned toward him. His good arm crept around her, and his lips met hers. "Ellen, Ellen," he whispered.

A moment later he released her, and, in spite of his command, she watched him, fascinated, as he climbed the ladder. Bullets whipped past him, but he seemed to bear a charmed life.

"Mel!" Ellen cried. "Don't let them see you!" Then she realized what a foolish thing she had said. Of course, they would see him when he reached the top of the tower.

The firing ceased as though by order, and Ellen looked out to see a group of men ride up to Cal. She recognized one as Bill

Sommers, the sheriff from Wimbleton.

"Cal Steele," she heard him say, "I arrest you for the murder of Bud Kelley, Wayne Rathburn, an' Harry Atwood. Lute Hodnette confessed the whole thing in writin', an' we got you dead to rights. Put up your hands."

"You're crazy!" Cal stormed as he faced the sheriff. "In there is your man. It's the gray rider, you damned fool. Him an' Hodnette is pullin' together."

For a moment the sheriff hesitated. Then he raised his open hand and came forward. "Don't shoot!" he called. "I'm findin' out what's goin' on around here, gray rider or no gray rider."

As he came forward, Cal whipped up his rifle and fired. The sheriff staggered and fell. Cal leaped into the saddle and dashed straight away over the prairie. A man fired, and then another, but Cal held straight on.

A hundred yards or more he went, lying close to the horse's back. Men were scrambling into saddles to follow, when there came the sharp crack of a rifle. Cal yelled, threw up his hands, wavered a moment, and then pitched to the ground.

Unseen by the ranchers, a thin line of men had crept up from the north — the battle

90

line of the nesters. They had fired the first shot at Cal Steele.

Ellen watched without moving as the ranchers drove back their horses and then lay flat on the ground. She knew most of them; some were her own men. She saw Tom Train firing a high-power rifle. Hank Trellis was by him.

The steady crashing of guns swept along the line. The nesters, led by a dozen hired killers, crept closer, firing as they came.

Mel was working feverishly, white of face, weak from pain and loss of blood. Ellen saw him force a bolt through a hole that connected two rods, and then climb slowly down the ladder.

Seizing a lever, he forced it far up. The great wheel at the top of the tower began to turn.

"Thank God," he murmured.

The firing continued, and the two opposing forces crept slowly forward. Mel staggered out of the tower, and the girl followed.

"Stay here, Ellen!" he cried. "I've got to stop that fight."

He dashed directly between the two lines of men. With a scream, Ellen sprang after him. She saw him throw up his arm and sink to the ground. Then he got to his feet and staggered forward.

In a moment she was at his side, her arm about him.

"Don't shoot!" she cried to the embattled men with a sob in her voice. "Oh, please don't shoot!"

The firing slackened. Mel stood on unsteady feet and gestured toward the tower.

"The range war is over!" he called. "There is water . . . enough for every ranch. Let the nesters have the valley an' the water holes. They'll raise hay an' grain an' vegetables for us all. Professor Hendricks has showed us how to bring water to the range!"

Gushing from a three-inch pipe in the side of the tower was a clear stream that gathered into a tiny pond in a low place in the ground.

"Well, I'll be a son-of-a-gun!" exclaimed Hank Trellis. "That danged professor was right again. Look at her rain!"

"There's nothing to fight about any more," Mel went on huskily. "The whole thing was a frame-up, anyway. Cal Steele shot those ranchers an' nesters, an' he did it for Hodnette. Both of 'em are dead an' gone to hell."

Without another word he pitched forward on his face. Ellen took his head into her arms, sobbing. Wondering men, nesters and ranchers, gathered about them.

Mel awakened in his own house, in his own bed. He gazed about him a moment, and then looked into the face of the girl who sat by his side.

"Ellen. . . ."

"Hush, dear," she cautioned as she put her fingers over his lips. "Doctor Abbott said you are to be very quiet. You've been close to death, but I knew you would live for my sake."

He closed his eyes and did not care to speak, for he was kissing the fingers that were pressed against his lips.

TRAIL DRIVER'S LUCK

For a week the noise of the trail herd had beat steadily upon the ears of Frazee — by day a muffled rumble of hoofs, a sound deep and thick as a wrapping of hot cotton; by night an incessant, dry bawling of thirst-tormented cattle. Now that he was away from the herd, he noticed with surprise that the vast sun-baked levels of the Mexican plain still had a silence like the end of time, or the peace of God.

Yet there was an unrest under the silence, a small stir somewhere in the far northeast, up by the Texas border. So small was that irritant under the quiet that it could almost be forgotten, like a touch of cactus dust on the skin. Only when you listened carefully, not breathing, could you be certain that to the northeast there were rifles popping, hundreds of them, in a straggling, shapeless battle.

That far-off rustle of gunpowder was very much in Frazee's mind, however, as he pulled up before the *rancho* of old Mario Contrera, just as the sun dropped behind the Sierra Madres.

The house of the Contrera *rancho* was long and commodious, and close to what ought to have been water; there were trees about it that had been set out long ago, and still lived, bent but mighty. Only the orchards behind had died utterly in the desert air. Old Mario Contrera himself, who now came out of the house to speak to Frazee, was beat like the trees, a man who had had unusual height, but had lost it in the twist of the years. His mustache was as gray as if it had been full of alkali, and he had a bitter, furrowed face.

"Contrera?"

"*Sí.*"

"My name's Frazee," said the rider. They spoke in Spanish. "Any water in your crick?"

"None."

"Any in . . . ?"

"None any place this side of the border itself."

Frazee shrugged, sweating silently. "There's clouds, though, there on the Sierras, Contrera."

"Always! Always!" Contrera's words burst out of him in passionate gusts. "All this devil's own summer, clouds hanging on the Sierras. But rain? Never! Never! And may God witness. . . ." He paused, and made a

95

hopeless gesture. "But . . . dismount, my friend. You must be thirsty and hungry."

"Gracias."

A ragged boy took Frazee's horse, and the two men walked together to the house. *"¿Como se va?"* said Frazee, flicking his eyes northeast.

Contrera was in no doubt as to what Frazee meant. What should anyone be asking about save the progress of the revolt? A dark emotion twisted old Mario's face as definitely as if it had been gripped by a hand. "Esparza stands like a bull. He still holds Ojo Caliente."

"Good!"

"You favor the revolt?"

"I favor Cherry Frazee," said the rider harshly, indicating himself. He chuckled, but in a way that Contrera perhaps did not like. "That dust . . . there in the southeast . . . my cattle are raising that. Five thousand damned gaunt, black-tongued, low-horned head! That is . . . they were five thousand three days ago. Naturally we're losing a few."

"I heard of your purchase, *señor.* And your drive up from Las Lomas. A valiant effort, my friend! I sympathize deeply."

"Sympathize?"

"This hell's own frying pan sucks the life

96

out of cattle as if they were tadpoles this year," said Contrera. "And to drive across it a starved and weakened herd. . . ."

Frazee laughed harshly. "I'll put them over the border in four days. And then . . . I've got hay at Loring, held for me until the Tenth of August. Hay and water will fix 'em up."

"Ah, Loring," said Contrera. His voice suggested that Loring was two miles beyond doomsday, as far as Frazee's cattle were concerned. "The cows are strong? You have plenty of men?"

"The cattle can hardly stand. I have two men with me, and loafers at that!"

Contrera tossed up his hands.

Frazee grinned. It had taken all he had, and all his credit, to tie up hay at Loring, and to buy — even for a song — a drought-punished herd deep down in old Mexico. This, however, was the sort of battle with urgency that he liked and was made for. Long chances were his natural roads to fortune, punishment his meat.

Contrera stood aside to let Frazee precede him through a cool, dark hall to an inner patio where the earth was kept firm and dustless by the water it drew up — and wasted — from an enormous cistern in the middle.

A girl was standing by the cistern head. Instantly, before he saw her face at all, Frazee knew who this was. He would have known the shadow of her shadow in hell, by just the bend of her head. The recognition took effect upon Frazee with a curious sense of shock, and immediately a small world of memories rushed through him like a flood released — so swift, yet so complete, as to be less a recollection than an emotion.

Francisca Contrera must have pretended not to hear them, for had she heard their approach, it would have been her duty to remove herself from the patio. Young Spanish women did not receive chance strangers, under the reign of the old ways. But Frazee knew women well enough to know that she had probably watched him ride up from a long way off. All that went through his head when he first saw her standing by the cistern head, her face turned away.

But that was in the background, a shadow. The important thing was that he had once held this girl in his arms, and kissed her well enough to make her remember him, once and for all. That had been at a *fiesta* that he had crashed at Monte Solano two years . . . three years ago, it must have been.

It had been a hard job, that day three years ago, to get a moment with her alone. So heavily chaperoned were those upper-class Spanish girls that few would have tried it. But Frazee had achieved perhaps three minutes alone with the girl in a shadowed walk that passed between a chapel and a clump of bamboo, and, before her *duenna* had come seeking her, he had seen all her pretended aloofness melt within the pressure of his arms.

Now, as she met his eyes for an instant in her father's patio, he saw the blood come into her face, and knew that she had had the same instant memory as he.

"Francisca," said Contrera, "let me present *Señor* Frazee . . . a drover." The last two words exploded ill-temperedly, telling Frazee that the introduction itself was intended as a rebuke. "My daughter," he said to Frazee with the same dryness. "We will excuse you, Francisca."

As she left them, she sent Frazee a glance full of laughter, such as women use to tease men who have had some small part of their favor, but will have no more. But what Frazee got out of it was a sudden conviction that he should have found out who she was, and searched her out again long ago. Until today, although he had remembered her often, he had never known her name.

A small wizened priest — or was it a friar?

— in a brown robe and an incongruous, little, stiff-brimmed straw hat joined them as Contrera provided wine, and presently food. After the inevitable peppered beans and meat there was white tequila, and with the closing of the hot dark door, Contrera became a little more expansive. As the old rancher monotoned the history of his misfortunes, what with repeated war and everlasting drought, Frazee found that he sat stark awake, where he would have expected to drowse. He had glimpsed a white *mantilla* at a patio window and knew that Francisca's eyes were upon him, and, when this was gone, he remained intensely conscious of the girl's presence in the house. He was listening and waiting, without knowing for what.

Mario Contrera seemed waiting, also. Behind the old man's monotone was an edge, as if he knew that something was about to happen, or that some word was to arrive that was going to change the meaning of everything on that hot, dry patio. Yet, when that word came, it was Frazee who was the more openly affected.

A rider, a blunt-faced swarthy man with Indian eyes, dropped off his horse before the outer door and, when he was admitted, stood fumbling his hat before Contrera.

"*Señor,*" — the messenger's words rattled like machine gunnery — "Esparza breaks! He falls back. His cavalry is God knows where. Ojo Caliente falls . . . he is beaten out of it. The army of the people is strung out for fifteen miles, and whoever is last, that is the rear guard, can protect themselves as they can. They say he cannot rally at the Moro as was thought. They say he will not stand now until Boleros . . . and, if God does not strike over his shoulder there, it is done. They say. . . ."

"You're sure of this?"

"*Señor,* I myself rode among the. . . ."

"How far is the retreat from Ojo Caliente?" Frazee demanded.

"*No lejos.*" That was the Mexican measurement: far, or not far. It might mean a day's march or a mile.

"Will the advance reach Boleros tomorrow night?"

"*Señor,* no. I am only here because I rode like the cinders of hell. Esparza. . . ."

"In two days, then?"

"As God wills."

Frazee smashed a furious fist down upon the table, and smoking words rumbled in his throat.

"Loring will never see the cattle of Frazee, *señor,*" said Contrera with weary assessment.

"In two days . . . three . . . there will be a twenty-mile wall of starving soldiery between. It is confiscation, *señor*."

"They'll have to come fast, then," swore Frazee. "I'm a long shot nearer Boleros than he is, and once my herd point sets hoof. . . ."

"I understood your cattle could hardly stand up," said Contrera.

"By God, I'll hold them up if I have to tail 'em up! If that herd stops here, it'll die where it stands. If only I had twenty. . . ."

"I have not a man to spare you," Contrera forestalled him.

Frazee's ears still drummed with the beating shuffle and bawl of that low-headed, spraddle-legged herd of his. To bring that herd to feed and water was to send his fortunes rocketing; to fail in this or to walk into confiscation at Boleros was to lose everything he had. The chance had been a slender one to begin with, and the odds were multiplying against him, yet, inarticulately, a sense of approaching triumph was upon him.

"I tell you this," said Frazee, his voice low and harsh. "Everything I have is in that herd of cattle. As you say, I cannot drive cattle through a rout of starving men. But if I'm first to Boleros, if I get that herd to the border. . . ."

"I have not a man to spare you," said Contrera again. "I'm sorry, my friend."

Frazee relaxed and grinned. *"Bueno,"* he said. "I have only two men, and those worthless, but I'll put four thousand of those five thousand head over the line!"

"Three men, with half-dead cattle, reach Boleros before Esparza? Impossible!"

"You'll see it done before the week's out."

Contrera shivered. "It's time for sleep," he said wearily. "A man is lucky to have a bed, and a roof over it, in times like these."

Alone in the little cell-like room assigned to him, Frazee stood looking out of the window. The brush-dotted plain lay flat and silent under hot, brassy stars, and the Madres were lost in the dark. The broken whisper beyond the northeast horizon seemed stronger now.

The yammer of a coyote drowned the ragged murmur of the distant guns, and he turned away. Slowly he stripped and sponged himself with tepid water from an earthen jar. Slowly, also, he pulled on his dusty clothes. He meant to be gone from there long before dawn.

Then, suddenly, he became acutely conscious again that the girl was somewhere near at hand, in the same household, under the same roof. She had been partly eclipsed, for a little while, by the necessities of his low-headed herd, but now his mind filled with her so completely that he could not stretch out on his bed, or attempt sleep.

He considered the lay-out of the *rancho*, and what he instantly pictured was the dry, withered orchard, divided by the dry serpentine bed of the river that had failed the trees.

Frazee stepped to his window. It was set with bars, but the first one that he tried cracked in his grip. Those bars must have been eaten into shells by the dry rot, for three or four of them almost went to dust as he broke them out with his hands, and stepped out into the open starlight of the plain.

Quiet-footed, he walked where the brown-leafed willows stood hot and lonely under the stars, marking the course of the waterless river. Then his eyes found a gleam of white, and he grinned, and the night was lonely no more.

In spite of his assurance, his certainty of himself, he had less than half expected that she would really be there. Yet she was there, waiting for him just as certainly as if it had been prearranged.

"Buenas noches," she murmured, her voice faintly cordial. "What are you doing here?"

"Came to talk to you," he said.

"And who asked you to do that . . . drover?"

"Now, pish, tush," said Frazee. He took her arm and clamped it against his side. Although she stiffened, she walked a little way farther from the house with him before she broke away.

"What was it you wanted to say?" the girl asked.

"I've been looking for you for three years," Frazee heard himself lie. "I don't know as you've been out of my mind an hour. And now I've run onto you again, I don't mean to leave you go."

She smiled up at him sidelong, queerly. "What do you mean by that?"

"I'm going to marry you."

They stood, silent, and the lonely Mexican night pressed nearer to them, hot and close. Then she looked at him curiously, and the cool poise seemed to go out of her. She began to laugh, almost silently, in her throat.

"What are you laughing at?" he demanded hotly.

"I was thinking of José."

"Who's José?"

"Did you ever see a man named José Exnicios?"

"No."

"I'm going to marry him the Tenth of August. We leave for the south in three days."

"The hell you are!"

"Why am I not?"

"Because before those three days are up, I'm coming after you. And you'll be ready to come with me, and you'll come with me . . . you hear?"

"And if I don't?"

"Then I'll take you, and I tell you this . . . it'll take more than the army of Mexico, and all hell, and you yourself to stop me."

A strange-voiced exclamation sounded startlingly, very close at hand, the breathy cry of an old man who comes sharply upon unutterable horror. Frazee, jerking up his head, saw the withered *padre*, shadowless and vague in the starlight. Then Francisca spoke.

"*Padre*," she began, her low voice unexpectedly clear and cool, "before you speak, before you judge. . . ."

The rotund figure stirred as if released from a spell. "You had better go in, my child."

Francisca obeyed. But first she leaned close for half a second to Frazee, speaking to him in a desperate whisper: "Within three days."

"Depend on me."

★ ★ ★

Shortly after daylight he found his herd, bedded eleven miles east of the Contrera *rancho*. That day Frazee did the work of three, changing horses at noon. His good *vaqueros* had deserted him for the fortunes of war — and his two remaining riders did little work, and that sullenly.

To see that every beast of that bawling, stumbling ruck moved steadily, never hurried, yet never lagging or wandering aside, would have been an insuperable job for many more men than Frazee, but it meant the difference between failure and success. He swarmed at it like a man inspired, a grim, grinning glow in his reddened eyes as he worried the stragglers. The whisper of rifle fire was stronger now, but still far to the east, and a faint haze on the horizon showed him where Boleros lay. He had never been surer in his life that he was close to a great victory. One day more. . . .

One day more to pass Boleros. Then the next day the two punk riders could muddle the herd along as best they could, for the chief danger would be past. That would leave Frazee free to kill a horse returning to the Contrera *rancho* for the girl. Francisca would be with him on the last short day, while they pressed the herd across the border to Loring, the goal that had been ahead of him for so long.

In a sense she was with him already. All that day they plugged across Contrera lands, and somehow that knowledge made her seem closer, as if her presence followed with him, like the sun.

Then, late in the afternoon, an Indian boy came riding a paint pony out of the south-west, whipping up side-and-side with his tie rope as he came in sight of the herd. He handed Frazee a tiny twisted wad of paper.

When Frazee had smoothed the paper out, he still had to stop his horse before he could decipher, with difficulty, the hesitant, sketchy little scrawl of three words that it contained.

"Never after tonight. . . ."

"The *señorita?*" he demanded.

"*Sí, señor.*"

"And what does she say?"

"Nothing, *señor.*"

"You don't know what she wants, or any-thing about it, but just this fool wad of paper?"

"Nothing, *señor.*"

"What night is she talking about?"

A blank stare was all he got out of that.

"Then . . . go hump that far bunch back into the show . . . pick 'em up, pick 'em up, but easy, see, or I break your. . . ."

"*Sí, señor!*"

Never after what night? Last night? If it was that, he could call it meaningless. But if never after *this* night — never what after when? If Francesca had only had the sense to. . . . But he knew that there was purpose in the ambiguity of those three words. She had to guard against interpretation, and so had written what should be meaningless to anyone but him. Ironically it was meaningless, also, to Frazee. But she had sent for him, he was pretty sure of that, and, if she sent for him, she had a reason. . . .

He wasted a futile moment reëstimating the two riders who held the point to its trail — two men of not much guts, sick and disgusted long ago with what they felt was a hopeless job. He knew with utter certainty that those two would never attempt to work the herd through for him alone, or succeed if they tried. If Frazee left the herd here, those worn-out cattle would scatter where they stood, to die presently in the unrelenting drought.

Never after tonight. . . .

Suddenly he saw that he was at the end of something. One thing or the other was over with and done.

He sat motionless on his stopped horse,

watching the mile-long struggle that the herd had become. They plugged along unevenly, a long welter of gaunt backs under a haze of dust. There in the slow hoofs of the cattle walked fortune. That herd was the tide which, "taken at the flood . . ." — Frazee himself was the very soul of that tide, the heart and guts of it that walked it on, as much a part of it as it was of him. And although his teeth were set hard into victory, the odds were heavy against him yet, and that was hardest of all: for the grip of utter urgency that was upon that herd held him with an all but resistless appeal.

The straggling tail of the herd passed him now, plodding doggedly with swinging heads. And finally the last gaunt cow, a staggering calf at her flank, paused and drew away from him slowly, slowly, as fortune was slipping out of his grasp.

He began to laugh, cracking his dry lips. This was the turning point of his career; yet he found himself without hesitation or doubt. Jauntily he kissed his hand to the herd, and unbuckled his chap strap to get at his money beneath. Then he signaled his riders in.

It was not long after midnight when Frazee, leading an extra horse, came within sight of the Contrera *rancho* again.

He sent the Indian boy ahead to see if anyone was up and, if possible, to tell Francisca that Frazee was here. Then, while waiting at a distance, a strange fear lay coldly across his shoulders, so ghastly pale and dead that house looked under the stars.

The boy was gone a long time, more than an hour, it seemed to Frazee. He came slinking out at last, so nearly invisible in the little light that Frazee did not see him until he was very close.

"The *señorita?*"

"I don't know."

"See anyone?"

"No one, *señor*. *El padre*. I saw the *padre*. He saw me, too, but I didn't want to talk to him. I ran out of his way."

"In hell's name, what took you all this time?"

"I looked all over. The horses are gone from the stable."

"Horses? What horses?"

"All the family horses, the horses kept at the house, although there is stock in the corral that. . . ."

Frazee swung into his saddle and put the pony to the house at a run. At the heavy front door he knocked twice, but when nothing moved within, he ran around the

111

house to the window of the room of the night he had spent there. Here he entered through the broken window bars, and went striding on into the patio.

The ubiquitous little *padre* was sitting by the cistern head, a lantern beside his feet.

"You, old man . . . where's Francisca?"

The *padre*'s voice shot back at him, unexpectedly harsh and sharp. "And who knows, if you don't?"

"What do you mean? Do you mean to say she's . . . ?"

"Her family left this morning . . . Contrera changed his plans for reasons that you should know best. But before they left, the *señorita* . . . she was gone."

"Gone where?"

"It's supposed," said the *padre* almost savagely, "that you took her!"

"So the family . . . ?"

"They thought you had ridden south. Naturally you wouldn't try to rejoin your herd under their very noses. They have gone southward in pursuit."

"*Padre*, listen . . . I never took her! I don't know anything about it!"

"You swear it?"

"Sure, I swear it!"

The little old man stood staring at Frazee with eyes like lancets. "What has happened

112

here, then?" he mumbled dimly.

Frazee seized the old man by the shoulders as if he would shake his brain awake. "Think, *padre* . . . where could she go? What could happen to her here?"

"I don't know . . . I don't know. . . ."

A silence fell upon them, as complete as if the world had turned still as the sky. Then softly, somewhere in a far wing of the house, Frazee heard a door open and close.

He snatched up the lantern and went running into the shadows of the still house, not calling out, but with quiet feet, trying to listen as he went.

In her own room, on her knees beside her bed, he found Francisca. She seemed afraid of him now, and hid her face in his shoulder and wept.

"Child, what's happened?"

"I wouldn't go south with them, I wouldn't go . . . but I had to trick them. I hid my saddle, and myself with it, and they thought I was gone. They're looking for me . . . and you . . . in Monte Solano, by now, I suppose. I knew you'd come. But you took a long time. . . ."

The *padre* came, following the lantern light, his slippers *slop-slopping* on the floor tiles. Francisca freed herself from Frazee's arms and stood quietly, facing the robed old man — tall and serene, and certain of herself, like a young-faced Madonna, except that there was an unMadonna-like smoldering fire behind the surface of her eyes.

"You are about to marry us, *padre*," said Frazee.

"But if that is impossible?"

"Then, by God, I'll take her anyway."

"But . . . if. . . ."

"Then I'll go with him," said Francisca.

The *padre* regarded them with miserable eyes. Then he said at last: "Stand here before the cross."

"Where's your saddle?" Frazee asked, when the *padre* was gone.

He could hardly hear her answer, her voice had turned so shaky and faint. "There's no need. . . . Isn't this our house tonight?"

Waking a short hour before dawn, Frazee strained his eyes against such blackness as he could not remember having seen before. There were no longer stars beyond the window bars, but the night had lost its silence, and the whole of the vast desert was filled with a new rush and moan of sound that at first he could not believe.

Gently he drew his arm from Francisca's sleeping head. Once clear, he reached the

114

window in a bound. A slash of water struck in through the jalousie and whipped wet across his face, bringing him broadly awake. For an instant more he stood incredulous, then with one sweep of his arm he knocked the rotted shutter out of the way, and stepped out into the downpour.

He spread out his arms to it, prayerfully letting the mild, big-dropped deluge run down his body in rivulets, and paste his hair down into his eyes. He was picturing to himself his wet-backed herd thirstily sucking up the saving water from rivulets and swales. She was sure enough his luck, luck past all believing! If he had pushed on, into the path of that hand-pressed retreat. . . .

In the whir and slat of the rain he was hearing the shuffle of numberless hoofs, and he knew that he was listening to prophecy, the rain's promise to him of mighty herds unborn.

THE LOAN OF A GUN

"Et?"

"Yup."

"It wouldn't surprise me none," said old Creaky Magruder, with that air of open amiability with which he had never deceived anyone yet, "if Kerrigan wouldn't appreciate the loan of a weepin."

The eyes of the two men by the fire flickered upward to Kerrigan's face, found he was not looking at them, and fastened there. It was a good poker face for a youngster of twenty, lean and smooth, with nothing readable in it except a pronounced obstinacy about the mouth. Kerrigan was gazing into the distances of the plain, where the shadow of the ranges had turned the quivering heat blaze to a misty welter of purples and mauve grays. Only the flat table tops of a far, tall mesa caught the last of the sunlight in a crowning stripe of gold.

Black dots out there at the foot of the mesa were cattle, but Kerrigan did not appear to be looking at them. For all those two

116

men could tell, he was thinking about the far adobe walls of Santa Fé and the laughter of dark-eyed girls behind latticed windows.

"Ain't he wearin' no weepin?" said Lute Gilmore. His voice affected innocence but poorly, for he was a man with a thick face and a thick head.

"Am I sittin' on a horse?" asked Kerrigan. He plucked a blade of grass, and chewed it meditatively.

"Looks like you'd be actin' sheriff now that Pop Waterman's dead," Magruder suggested cautiously.

"Looks like it," Kerrigan agreed.

His eyes, still speculative, turned from the distance to the two men by the fire, and casually, as if by coincidence, first the eyes of Creaky Magruder and then those of Lute Gilmore dropped to the orange coals. With neither liking nor dislike, Kerrigan studied the greasy clothes and thin beard of Magruder. That sly, presuming amiability almost made Kerrigan sorry for the old ruffian. As for Lute Gilmore, he had a strong back. So did horses.

His eyes returned to the dimming reaches of the plain, but he was not thinking about girls or Santa Fé. Before him, beyond the little huddle of bright coals at his feet, the slopes fell away through piñon pine and scrub juniper to the New Mexican flats, but behind him the steep-shouldering Cimarrón Range piled skyward, black with pine and spruce, gray-green with aspen. Kerrigan was seeking a man whom he believed to be hidden somewhere in the raw, rugged gashes of those slopes.

"Have they caught Joey Greaves?" Magruder asked.

"Not that I know of."

"Le' see . . . last Monday was it? . . . he shot Pop Waterman in the back. Monday? The Saturday before, by damn!"

If Kerrigan understood Magruder's implied criticism of the dead sheriff's deputies, he took no offense. "Seems a long time," he agreed, "five days."

"Yes, I reckon," said Magruder.

Lute Gilmore said nothing. He hardly ever did.

"I kind of thought," Magruder went on, "you'd go south with one o' them posses that was chasin' Greaves. I suppose he made old Mexico, all right. But I kind o' thought you'd've gone."

"Did you?" asked Kerrigan.

"Uhn-huh." Magruder lit a pipe, and rocked away, slowly and noisily. "But then," he suggested, "maybe you didn't think Greaves went south."

"Maybe I didn't," Kerrigan agreed.

"Maybe," said Magruder, thin, incredibly impudent slyness creeping into his voice, "you come lookin' for him over here."

"Maybe," said Kerrigan again. "Don't doubt yourself so much, Magruder."

Old Creaky shot him a glance. "Pity you didn't find him," he commented. "I suppose you'll be headin' back Wolf Springs way, now?" Kerrigan said nothing, and presently Magruder went on: "You're about the first feller I ever seen sheriffin' without a gun, Kerry . . . no . . . I seen one other once. Mister Bob MacPherson. Whopper. Bald head with a dent in it. Feller put the dent in with a flatiron from behind him when Bob was playin' poker. Bob up and hit him with a chair. It run along with him sheriff quite a piece. But finally some fellers couldn't stand him no more. So they shot him."

Kerrigan was familiar with the yarn; in those days everyone in the country had heard of Bob MacPherson, the sheriff who owned no gun.

Magruder waited for Kerrigan to say something, but was disappointed. "I suppose, though," he said at last, "you anyways got a gun in your saddlebag."

"No," said Kerrigan. "Worries you, doesn't it? Well, my horse stumbled crossing a white-water crick, and I lost it." The truth, only the truth, the last thing Magruder would expect. "Now you know. Feel better?"

"Didn't want to seem pryin', Kerry."

"No, I suppose not. Still, glad to know, aren't you? I wouldn't lie to you, Magruder."

"Never said you would, Kerry," the old reprobate blared heartily.

Magruder and Lute Gilmore were riders from the Circle Hook. It was an outfit that had bitterly opposed the election of Pop Waterman, now dead by Joey Greaves's gun, and the Circle Hook had been Greaves's home outfit. Kerrigan was speculating now as to how far these birds of a feather would go in behalf of their man. He knew that they would aid his escape in any convenient way. He did not think, however, that they would openly buck the law.

For two days Kerrigan had lain on the edge of Mesa Gallina, fifteen miles away, smoking cigarettes and watching the crevices of the uprearing Cimarróns. He knew every groove of that range. Given a wisp of smoke he could, at thirty miles, almost name the men who cooked there or, failing the name, tell where he had come from, what was his business, and where he was going next.

Kerrigan had not shared the general belief that the killer of Pop Waterman had made a run for old Mexico. Just as a truth was a better concealment than a lie, so sometimes it was darkest under the light, even in that sparsely settled day — if a man had friends. Kerrigan was first deputy — acting sheriff, now that Waterman was dead, but he had let the silent fury of the volunteer posses go boiling down the Chihuahua trail without him. Greaves's logical hide-out, he reasoned, would be somewhere on the near watershed of the Cimarróns.

Patiently he had combed the ragged slopes with his eyes, testing and retesting his knowledge of the terrain. Across the miles the parched clear air showed him every outline of the individual trees, tiny as moss fragments, but incredibly distinct. And at last a far away ghost in the branches of the pines had told him that what he had guessed was true: a man was camped where no man — but one — had any reason to be. Across the blaze of the plain and into the foothills rode Kerrigan with the stir of the manhunt in his blood; and then that half-wit accident had deprived him of his gun.

It was Kerrigan's second misfortune, although he blamed himself now that he should stumble on these particular men. He had seen them, from far away on the mesa, early in the day. Working stock, apparently, or getting ready to — near the foot of the Arroyo Hondo, up which he must now strike in the pursuit of Joey Greaves. He had taken them for men of the Bar K, since this was Bar K range more than any other.

It was certain now that, if he borrowed a gun from these men, they would make every effort to warn Greaves, and it was unlikely that they could fail. His mistake in displaying himself to men of the Circle Hook, apparently camped for the particular purpose of covering the fugitive, made further pursuit useless, unless. . . .

"I wisht we could loan you a weepin," said Magruder. "You know how it is in workin' stock. I dunno as we. . . ."

"Won't need any," said Kerrigan.

He turned casually, inspected the cinch of his pony, and prepared to mount.

"Pushin' back to Wolf Springs, I suppose?" Magruder couldn't keep his questions off of other people's business. It would be the death of him someday.

"Nope," said Kerrigan. He returned old Magruder's questioning gaze until the other dropped his eyes. "I'm goin' out and round up Greaves with my bare hands. Want to come?"

Truth, nothing but the truth, that was the stuff to off trail old Magruder.

"Take a drink for me," said Magruder, "when you get to Wolf Springs."

> **Four cards to the boss of**
> **the Circle Hook,**
> **Two cards more to the Chinese cook,**
> **Whole new hand for Charlie McGraw.**
> **Gambler guesses that he won't draw.**
> **The cowboy, he was topped again,**
> **And they all went seven hands 'round.**

Kerrigan sang softly to himself as the bay horse picked his way steadily up what passed for a trail beside the steep Arroyo Hondo.

> **Three to the man with burrs**
> **in his beard,**
> **Two to this man whose hand is feared,**
> **Three to the man whose nose is blue.**
> **Gambler guesses one card will do.**
> **The cowboy, he was topped again,**
> **And they all went seven hands 'round.**

Up and up, while the faint keen smell of the piñons was replaced by the heavier resinous odor from the dark snags of spruce and fir, until at last a round-topped pillar of rock showed faintly blue in the starlight above the spruce, and Kerrigan turned off.

Half an hour later a distinct smell of frying grease came into the downcañon breeze. Kerrigan felt the ribs of his horse suddenly expand, and jerked down the beast's head in time to turn a proposed whinny into a grunt. He dismounted, and picketed the horse.

Ten minutes' walk brought him into sight of a gleam of firelight through the trees, well-hidden, unexpectedly close before he came upon it. A short stalk completed his reconnaissance. Kerrigan's reasoning had been right.

Greaves was cooking. It was late to be cooking supper, but the smell of venison suggested that the murderer of Pop Waterman had been hunting at some distance, and had just returned with his fresh meat. Kerrigan thanked his stars, and a new plan quickly formed in his head. He retreated to a distance of a hundred yards, and advanced once more, this time noisily.

**Three to the man with the homely pan,
Four to the boy with the worthless hand,
Three to the man in the high silk hat.
None to the gambler . . .**

he's standing pat.
The cowboy, he was topped again,
And they all went seven hands 'round.

The song drifted gently across the night, over the bushes, through the spruce. When Kerrigan came into the little glade where the fire snapped, no man was there. Casually Kerrigan went on with his song.

Three to the man with the
green glass eye,
One to the man that's always dry,
Four to the man that's troubled
with fleas.
Gambler guesses that he'll play these.
The cowboy, he was topped again,
And they all went seven hands 'round.

He dragged the hot-handled frying pan, containing an enormous venison steak, off the coals. Rummaging around, he found salt, with which he sprinkled the venison. There was no bread of any kind in evidence, but he found coffee, and fresh water in a two-quart canteen. He scoured the pan with grass, and in the same pan that had fried the meat set coffee on the fire.

"Come on in, Greaves. Supper's done."

No reply.

Something of the uneasy feel of a man who talks at emptiness was upon Kerrigan as he called out again: "Come on, you, Greaves. Do I eat by myself?"

Silence again, until Kerrigan began to feel that he had made some sort of mistake. He listened now for the sound of a distant horse, but the silence remained intact. Then suddenly, almost immediately behind him: "Put up your hands. If you turn your head, I'll plug you."

Kerrigan's hair rose with the nearness of the hard, cool voice. This was as he had hoped and planned, yet the muscles of his back crept. He had not expected, for one thing, that the command would come from so extremely close. It flashed through his mind that Greaves must have executed his disappearance by simply slipping into the arms of the nearest spruce, and stepping two branches off the ground.

"Hi, Greaves," said Kerrigan.

"Are you going to put 'em up?" said the voice from behind, with more menace this time.

Kerrigan began to slice through the steak with his opened knife.

"Don't be so dumb, Joey," he said. "You see I ain't armed."

"I do, like hell," said Greaves, stiffly argumentative.

Kerrigan raised his hands over his head, stood up, and slowly pivoted on his heels. "You see now."

"Chuck that knife away."

Kerrigan flung the knife twirling, and it stuck upright in the ground on the other side of the fire.

"Where'd you leave your gun?" came Greaves's voice.

"Didn't bring any."

The silence seemed to think that over.

"How many's with you?" demanded the voice from the spruce at last.

"Not a one, Greaves."

"You're lying, Kerry."

"All right. Figure it that way."

"Where's your horse?"

"I hid him," said Kerrigan.

"Where?"

"Go to hell, Greaves. Think I want to be set afoot in the middle of everything?"

"I guess you'd rather be set afoot than planted."

"Don't know as I would. Make up your mind, Joey. You know damned well, to begin with, you ain't goin' to leave here without anything to eat. I come up here unarmed and alone, because I want to talk to you.

127

And I can do some thinkin' as well as eatin' before you drag your freight. I could have brought a gang up and surrounded you. I could have had the drop on you tonight. You better come out here and do some listening."

"How do I know I won't be plugged when I step into the light?"

"If that's the way I've got it fixed, why did I chase you out of the light in the first place?"

Another interval of silence. Then a grumble: "Think you're all-fired smart, don't you?" Then a swishing of evergreen boughs, and Joey Greaves skirted the circle of firelight, and appeared on the side opposite Kerrigan.

Greaves was slender and young. In his skin was the suggestion of a swarthiness that intimated to any Southwesterner that there might be in this man some part of *mestiza* blood, but his eyes were blue. They were small and almost ominously wide-set — and the direction of their gaze was curiously expressionless, as if they were opaque, so that the gaze of another could not strike through them to make them flinch.

"All right," he said, "what's the game?"

Kerrigan could see that this man was puzzled, angered, and worried. "Let's have something to eat," the deputy suggested.

Without taking his eyes from Kerrigan, Greaves leaned his rifle across his saddle, and stepped into the open of the firelight. His .44 was in his right hand. For a few moments he stood motionless, as if waiting, not tense, but ready; and, although his eyes remained on Kerrigan, the deputy could see that the killer was listening.

"Just as I told you," said Kerrigan presently. "You see? Nothing happens."

Greaves's rather stiff-skinned face cracked into a quick grin, then returned to immobility. "Maybe you're a bigger fool than I thought," he conceded. "Set down back there. Pretty far from the fire."

The coffee was bubbling in the frying pan, and with his left hand Greaves pulled it off. He picked up the meat that Kerrigan had cut, and flung the deputy a piece. They ate with their hands, tearing the meat apart with their teeth. Whatever he did, Greaves kept hold of the gun in his right hand, and mostly his wide-set eyes were on Kerrigan, stolid, expressionless, like the eyes of a turtle on a rock.

Now, Kerrigan was thinking, was the time for him to make his play. He was thinking of old Bob MacPherson, the sheriff without a gun, the man who had become a legend in the Southwest before he had been killed, at last, under circumstances in which a gun would have done him no good. Kerrigan had talked with that man once. MacPherson had grown old by then, dried up by the desert air so that his height was minimized, and he looked wiry and small. A man with thin hair, a gray mustache, and a slow, mild eye. "You can do it if you think you can . . . I haven't carried a gun for years."

That was all you could get out of him about how he was able to bring in hard-boiled desperadoes time and again, with apparently nothing in his favor but the power of human debate. Kerrigan was trying to imagine, now, how MacPherson had turned the trick. He had always wanted to try something like that; his chance was ready now.

The deputy spoke casually with his mouth full: "You certainly made some bad mistakes, Joey," he suggested. Unconsciously his voice imitated the slow rhythms of Bob MacPherson as an old man. "I never see such bum reasonin'."

"Yeah?" said Greaves.

"Looks like you ought to have headed over the Sangre de Cristo Range first off. East, that would've been the ticket. Of course, that wouldn't have been no good unless you done it quick. Pop Waterman had a pile of friends over that way. They shot a feller over that way the other day because they thought he was you. He'll live, I heard. They've camped in the passes though, now. . . ."

Greaves snorted.

"Failin' that," Kerrigan went on, "you might have made it by bustin' off through the Conejos country. Too late now. They know by this time you're in the Cimarrón Range. Nothin's comin' out of it, except by horse race, any more. Some of the Lazy M shagged a feller fifteen miles the other day, thinkin'. . . ."

"Lazy M?" Greaves cut in. For a moment he stopped chewing.

"Yeah, I know you worked for that outfit once. But when it comes right down to it, most fellers get mad, nowadays, when somethin' like this happens. Well, failin' to cut north about did it, I guess. South and west, they had a heap of fast horses runnin', durin' the past week. Pretty hard to get clear, any place so open. Of course, the Black Range might've turned the trick, but even so. . . ."

Greaves, he could see, was puzzled behind that small-eyed, wide-set stare. What

Greaves wanted to know was what Kerrigan was about. The deputy's report of conditions was not making much impression, he could see.

"How come you," Kerrigan went on, "to take an old snake like Creaky Magruder into your confidence? That old reprobate. . . ."

Greaves said: "If that old scoundrel has. . . ."

"As for Lute," said Kerrigan, "that hoople's understandin' is obstructed. Still, I expect runners is hard to find. This thing of shootin' a man from behind. . . ."

"I never done so," said Greaves.

"No?"

"I walked into his office. Pop Waterman set with his back to me. As I come in, somebody shot through the window. Pop jerked like he was hit. But he turned around, shootin' as he turned. He shot twice, at me, see? Well" — Greaves's voice was slow, and he pronounced the words distinctly, as if he were trying to explain something to a half-wit — "I pulled and plugged him. Only thing come to mind to do, and he fell over. My shot was in front, after he'd fired on me twice."

Kerrigan thought that over. "Pop was hit once," he said. "From behind. There wasn't any shot from in front . . . except one in the wall."

Greaves stared at him, not chewing for

some time. "Then I never hit him," he said. "Say . . . how many shots was fired, accordin' to the fellers around there?"

"I could prove anywheres from three to six," said Kerrigan. "But . . . most of 'em said four, an' that's a fact."

"See?" said Greaves. "I fired one shot. Pop shot twice. The shot that done it come in the window, like I said."

There was a long silence, while they finished the meat.

"Look, Joey," said Kerrigan, unconsciously imitating old MacPherson again, "there ain't a human way to bust out of this range alive. That's what I come to tell you. Go back with me. You say you never done it. All right. I'd just as soon believe you. You come back with me, and I'll see you get a fair trial."

It was the climax of his play. Upon Greaves's reaction depended his success or his failure. There were too many unexplained factors in Greaves's story to render it credible. He didn't want to ask Greaves, at this time, how it had happened, for example, that he had walked into Pop Waterman's office with a drawn gun. Some things like that. The thing now was to get the killer of Pop Waterman down there to the Wolf Springs jail. The wide-set eyes were upon him, steady and expressionless. *This was easy,*

133

said Kerrigan to himself.

Then Greaves's stiff-hided face cracked in the same mirthless grin that Kerrigan had seen before. "You poor fool," he chuckled. "You poor sap-headed fool. This is rich. Some Bob MacPherson stuff, huh? Well, get this through your weak head . . . you nor no other man is goin' to take me into Wolf Springs, not you, nor the Lazy M, nor all the 'punchers in this country. Not tonight, nor tomorrow, not next week, nor no time, not living and not dead."

"Have it your own way," said Kerrigan. He shifted on his heels as if he were about to get up.

"Siddown!" Greaves told him. "You ain't goin' no place. When I get ready, you're goin' to show me where your horse is. I need another. I'm hopin' that somewhere in the meantime you'll make an off-color move, because a dead sheriff is twice as pretty as one of 'em afoot. Maybe I'll take a pop at you anyway. I ain't quite decided yet." Slowly he drank the coffee, staring over the pan's edge.

"All right, all right," said Kerrigan. He yawned and stretched and took off his hat as though to cool his head. The hunted man seemed to take this for a hostile move.

"If you got a gun in that hat. . . ."

"You see I ain't. Only. . . ."

"Only what?"

"Why, I thought some o' hittin' you with it."

"With what?"

"My hat."

Greaves spat.

"Remember one thing," said Kerrigan, "I ain't lied to you yet." Slowly, sadly, he sang under his breath.

**Give me the man with the
hard-boiled shirt,
Two to the herder all caked with dirt,
The Mex night wrangler
is standing pat.
And the gambler has seen
enough of that,
The cowboy, he was topped again,
And they all went seven hands 'round.**

He was squatting on his heels, his hat in one hand, the other dangling empty over the knees. Greaves was slowly oscillating the frying pan, working the grounds into the angle of the bottom, like a miner panning sand. Kerrigan's eyes stared vaguely into the ebbing coals of the fire.

**Three to the man with the broken nose,
Four to the man in expensive clothes,**

Three to the lad that slept in the ditch. One to the gambler. . . .

The eyes that seemed to watch the fire saw Greaves raise the coffee pan. For an instant the pan was in front of the killer's face as he flipped the last of the dregs into his mouth; for a second, the split part of a second, the expressionless eyes were obscured.

Kerrigan's hat shot across the interval and slammed against the bottom of the pan. Greaves's gun cracked, its flame an instant yellow spike against the dark in back. Simultaneously the dirt jumped just in front of the spot where Kerrigan had squatted, and the voice of the gun was prolonged an instant by the whine of the ricochet.

Headlong across the fire Kerrigan cannoned upon his man. The hammer of the gun, falling again, bit into the thumb muscles of his left hand. Greaves's teeth closed into the side of his neck, and a hook-like thumb was gouging for his eyes. Too tightly gripped together to knee or slug, the two men rolled over and over, and their shirts smoked from the fire's crushed coals.

Creaky Magruder was belly to the Blue

Line Bar at Wolf Springs. The bartender had tried to work him into conversation, for trade was slack, and bartenders are sociable men. Magruder, however, was taciturn. "I don't know what this country is coming to," he said at last. "So bustin' full of damn' young fools."

"What's the matter now?" said the full-bosomed apron behind the bar.

"I seen Kerrigan the other day," said Magruder, as if that statement alone were sufficiently to the point.

"There's been some sour talk about him," the bartender offered, leaning forward confidentially. "It ain't took well that he turned up missin' just when the posses was startin'. Startin' after Joey Greaves," he amplified, "that shot Pop Waterman."

"Well," said Magruder testily, "I guess I knew who shot who around here."

"Some fellers come in that ain't heard it," said the bartender equably. "Some fellers don't seem to hear about things."

"I ain't one of 'em."

"Well, anyway," the bartender repeated lamely, "it wasn't well took."

"You said that before," Magruder murmured. "What I say is, this Kerrigan oughtn't to be let run around loose."

"Wheredja see him?"

137

"He ought to be shet up," Magruder murmured. "I seen him up by the Cimarrón Range. He'd fell in a crick and lost his gun. Or so he said. I could anyways see he had fell in a crick. Deputy fell in a crick! Geez! And lost his gun. . . ."

"It's terrible," agreed the bartender, "the way things goes, sometimes."

A queer light came into Magruder's eyes. He was cocking an ear to the door. From the street came the bars of a mournful song.

Three to the man with the broken nose,
Four to the man in expensive clothes,
Three to the lad that slept in the ditch.
One to the gambler, the son-of-a-gun.
The cowboy, he was topped again. . . .

A man, recognizable by general shape and voice as Kerrigan, came a little stiffly through the door. His left hand was bandaged with strips of a shirt not his own, so was his head, as if one ear might have been held in place thereby.

"By golly," said the bulging apron, "looks like somebody's been beatin' you about the head and chist."

"The first thing I need," Kerrigan said, "is a drink."

The bartender supplied it.

"Ain't that," wavered Creaky Magruder, "the gun that . . . ?"

"That's one I borried off of Greaves," said Kerrigan. "He ain't goin' to need it till after the trial."

"Greaves," Creaky began again.

"He's over in the jail," Kerrigan supplied. "MacPherson was right. Peaceful ways is best."

"Peaceful!" the bartender exploded. "You look like. . . ."

"At the crucial minute, somethin' occurred to me," said Kerrigan. "Thinkin' back, it seemed like to me MacPherson had a powerful sprinkling of scars for a peaceful man."

The bartender was avid: "Whatja do?"

"Creaky," said Kerrigan, "did I ever lie to you yet?"

"Not this trip," Magruder admitted.

"Coffee," Kerrigan told them, "was the undoin' of Joey Greaves."

"You flang coffee in his eyes?" the bartender suggested.

"I wouldn't lie to you," Kerrigan assured him. "He flung it in his own eyes."

"Geez!" moaned Creaky Magruder. He went reeling for the door.

EYES OF DOOM

On their fourteenth trip together, Tom Snair finally got his break. For more than two hundred miles the six-horse wool wagons had been crawling over the black lava-speckled desert, and an isolation, constant, inescapable, oppressive, had bound the two drivers together. Tom Snair could not remember all his reasons for hating Grogan; reason had ceased to count in the blind fury the other driver roused in him. It would have been easy a few years ago, he was thinking, to start a shooting scrape and have his chance at that broad, grinning face. But nowadays they wore no guns, and murder was generally called by its right name. Snair, in the depths of his poisoned soul, was afraid of a rope.

Today, as Snair looked ahead into emptiness from his seat on the lead wagon, he could hear Grogan, singing to himself on the second wagon. That cheery noise made Snair curse; he had to keep reminding himself that the crazy singing which followed him across the desert was really his own doing, and represented a minor success. For Snair knew that he could only wait for a sneaking chance to do for Grogan, and all he could do, while he waited, was to play on Grogan's weakness for corn whisky.

Then as his drag surged up out of the crossing of a dry coulée, a raw swing horse shied, and Snair was jerked up. On a boulder by the trail sat an old man. His hat was pulled down over his eyes, shadowing all but his ragged beard. At his feet crouched a black and gray dog.

"Give me a ride into town, mister!" The old man's voice was faint and hesitant.

Snair did not answer, but cracked his blacksnake over the lagging wheelers and plodded on. He was already fifty yards past when he became aware that Grogan had pulled up and was parleying with the stranger. In incidents that had to do with Grogan, Snair flared up less upon occasion than upon opportunity, and he flared up now. For Snair — although he did not think of it — was probably the only man in the sheep country who would refuse another a lift.

He could not see around the huge brown pile of wool bags, so he hauled in his team, jumped down, and went striding back. The old man was moving to climb aboard Grogan's wagon.

Snair's voice split the quiet: "Here . . . get away from that! We got a top load here. This ain't no passenger train!"

Grogan's answer came readily, easy with contempt: "Go lay an egg!"

The quarrel, smoldering always, even under Grogan's cheerfulness, was suddenly a burning fire. The old man stumbled backward, away from the wagon; he stood listening as Snair begged Grogan to get down and fight, his maledictions working upon Grogan as a sixteen-foot blacksnake works over a bogged team.

Grogan stood up on the footboard, swaying dizzily with Snair's whisky. Undoubtedly it was his intention to come down off that wagon fighting, as, in his carefree, reckless manner, he had come down many and many a time before. But this time, as he jumped, the toe of his boot caught in the ratchet of the brake. His great body, arms outflung, came spread-eagling through the air, and, as Snair stepped back, Grogan landed head-on in that broken black lava. His skull struck with a muffled crack.

Snair charged upon the inert, awkwardly sprawled body, but Grogan did not move again. For a moment Snair stood over him, dazed. He looked toward the old man, but the old man was hurrying away, his retreat covered by the gray dog that kept looking back with raised hackles. Snair called out, but the old man hurried faster, up the hill toward a lonely cabin. Turning back, Snair made certain that Grogan was dead.

When Snair had shaken the bewilderment from his brain, a slow exultation came into him, for he realized now that he had killed this man just as certainly as if he had picked up that black chunk of lava and hurled it. It was the tangle-foot whisky that had pitched Grogan to his death — Snair's whisky. Aided by a mysterious and kindly fate, he had done for his enemy in the most desirably possible way — a way so handily perfect that no word could ever be raised against him. Snair grinned grotesquely as he lifted the limp body to his own wagon and jammed it among the wool sacks. Deliberately, but very merrily, he unhooked the horses from the second wagon and tied them behind his own. Town was eight miles away.

Occasionally, as he drove on, he turned and looked back at Grogan's legs protruding from the wool sacks, helpless, tragically absurd, and he smiled again. Snair did not even have to shape a story. The simple truth would clear him, and he had a witness to that truth.

In town he brought his wagon to a halt before the hotel where he could ask for the coroner. Loafers from the hotel perched around as he lifted Grogan's body to the ground with regretful care. Many of those loafers knew him. More had known Grogan, and there was a murmur of honest grief. Grogan's face showed a curious, contorted smile until someone put a handkerchief over it, changing it to a blotch of blue color on the dust.

Will Durner, town marshal, pushed through the crowd. "What's happened?"

Readily, concealing his exultant satisfaction, Snair told his story. Will Durner shook his head. "I don't know about that," he objected. "Did you and Grogan ever have any trouble?"

"I should say not . . . ," Snair began, but someone in the crowd protested hostilely. They did not believe him. He could see in the dark faces, as they pressed close, that they thought he had struck Grogan down. But he faced them, confident and easy under their scrutiny. "There was an old man there by the trail," he said. "He saw it all happen."

Durner was puzzled. He remembered the shack eight miles out; prospectors stayed there sometimes. "I guess we'd better go on out and talk to him," Durner decided.

As Snair, riding on the marshal's buckboard, finally pointed out the shack, he was glad that half the town was following behind. "That dump up yonder," he indicated. "There he is."

The old man was squatting against the adobe wall, his dog beside him.

"Yes, sir. I stood by while them two fellers had their row," he told them.

"You saw Grogan fall and hit his head on a rock," Snair insisted.

"No. I just heard you cuss him out. You dared him to come down. Then there was a yell and a whacking noise. . . ."

Snair lunged toward the old man, but a dozen hands held him back. "You're lying!" Snair shouted. "You saw. . . ."

But the old man was staring past him with pale, meaningless eyes. His voice was distant, innocent, full of doom. "No, mister, I didn't see anything. I'm stone blind."

TOMBSTONE'S

DAUGHTER

"Gumption," said Tombstone, "sure as hell, is one of the things that has went to work and backslid on us."

He drew back his mustache to shoot tobacco juice at a pad of cactus twenty-three feet from the ranch house door at which he sat, missed, and leaned forward a little to squint suspiciously at the cactus, as if he thought it must have moved. Then he returned his gaze to the far, square-hewn horizon of the New Mexico mesas.

Nosey Tolley looked at Tombstone, but said nothing. He was aware that the backslid gumption referred to was Billy Dwight, his twenty-two-year-old employer. But Tolley's bottle nose was weather-beaten by more decades on the open range than he would have admitted, and he had the hog-tied loyalty to his employer that is peculiar, among cowboys, to those superannuated figures who don't know where the next job is coming

146

from. If Nosey agreed with Tombstone, he was going to keep it to himself.

Tombstone had been waiting for Billy Dwight for forty minutes. He did not fidget, or chew his ore-sample of a mustache. But Tolley did. The boss of the neighboring Bar Hook was a person of property and influence in those parts. Also, he was capable of a repressed lethal ferocity, the quality of which nobody cared to poke into any more. Billy Dwight was certainly in no position to keep Tombstone's sort of people waiting.

"Thing of the past," growled Tombstone speculatively. "Gone to blazes with the rest of the country."

Tolley, whose mind had wandered, looked surprised, for he conceived that Tombstone had made a personal confession. "Who?" he inquired mildly.

Tombstone favored him with a slow examination — not a glare, but something more ominous.

"I mean which," corrected Tolley hurriedly.

"Gumption!" snapped Tombstone.

"Oh!"

Nosey Tolley could sense the hostility piling up behind the mask of hardened leather that passed for Tombstone's face. If Tombstone could have seen what was

147

causing Billy Dwight's present delay, the hostility would have exploded into something not safe to innocent bystanders. If the cautious Tolley could have seen, he would probably have mounted on the gallop and hit for the hills.

At the moment, five miles away and around the shoulder of Snag-Tooth Mesa, Billy Dwight was riding with Tombstone's daughter. That daughter of Tombstone's could have made any youngster forget that he had a special appointment with the old snorter himself. She was letting her hair grow again, so that it was loose almost to her shoulders, and it was coffee brown, with a gold shimmer in it when the sun struck it. Her eyes were dusky gray, with a sidelong twinkle that could be humorous to the point of exasperation.

Visible on that range were the white-faced, low-headed cattle that he had ridden over here to see. Their hips stuck up and their ribs showed, and a few of them were even making an attempt to graze that heat-blazing dusty land that seemed to have turned to sheer desert under the scorch of the three-year drought. Those were what was left of Dwight's cattle, which he had inherited from his father four years ago. They were in pretty bad case, just now. But Billy Dwight, riding knee to knee with Tombstone's daughter, lost his eyes in the misty wind-blown tangle of her hair.

He could forget old Tombstone, almost forget the drought-strangled herds, while his eyes were on the subtle curve of the girl's throat. And when she turned her head so he could see her eyes, as vividly refreshing as the water that did not exist on the range any more, he could forget more than that: he could forget where he was, or his name.

"Cows don't look so good, Billy."

"Nope," said Dwight, "they don't."

"I'm afraid not many of them are going to make it, Billy."

"Nope," said Dwight again. "They aren't."

"When do you drive?"

"Tomorrow. We're the last pickup in the pool. The other twenty thousand head will make it here tonight . . . to judge by the dust. Ham Harris rode up here yesterday to see if we was all set."

"How many you going to drive?"

"A thousand head," he said slowly.

"Billy, there aren't a thousand head that can walk it!"

"I'll have to take the loss," he admitted.

Over beyond the near-broken horizon

they could see the faint, long haze of dust that marked the dragging approach of the twenty thousand cattle of the pool. The hopes of half a dozen cattlemen were in that gaunt, staring-eyed herd, small cattlemen that the three-year drought had laid flat on their backs. There was little water or food up and down the length of the southern range.

Foresighted heads had spent the snowless winter lining up the long chain of pastures that would enable them to make their last, forlorn-hope drive to a country of better feed. Pasturage came high, these days, with the open range well-filled and rapidly succumbing to the fence. Hardly a one of them would own a calf that he could call his own if the drive failed to save the remnants of their stock.

"Billy," Jane's throat was tight. She could picture as well as any cattleman among them the gaunt-hipped carcasses that would litter that trail of little hope, each marking for some cattleman a diminished opportunity to survive. "Billy . . . can you get five hundred head out of it?"

"I doubt it, Jane. If I do, I'll figure I've whipped the no rain."

"Can you do it?"

"Maybe."

If Dwight saved that remnant of his herds, he had a long, uphill fight ahead of him at best, while the wrecked land, desperately overgrazed in the drought, was nursed back into coverage again. And if he saved nothing — complete poverty — as if all the years of his father's life had been brought to nothing.

"Mortgaged to the hilt, Billy?"

"Right up to the eyes."

"Horse herd melted down?"

"Not much left, Jane."

"Ranch house fallen down yet?"

"I ain't been back for two hours. I could use a load of lumber and some nails."

He had sent his eyes out over the range for a moment, and she turned to look at his face, clean-shaved, quiet — and everlastingly, almost annoyingly, hopeful. She wondered how it was that he could conceal so well the strain, the twisting fear of complete defeat that must be behind it. Or was there behind it any fire at all? The Dwights didn't have gumption, as Tombstone understood the word. But the youngster was game; they couldn't deny him that.

"Dad's waiting for you," she reminded him. "If he hasn't ridden off. He doesn't think much of waiting for folks, Dad doesn't."

"Oh, he's waiting all right," said Dwight with an ironic confidence.

"Billy," said Jane suddenly, "why don't you sell out to him? Even now, you could just about name your price . . . you know what store he sets by his notion of a sightly ranch. He's wanted your ninety sections ever since I can remember. He thinks. . . ."

"Seems like he pretty near has enough," said Dwight, "what with his water. . . ."

"I know. But you know how hard these old-timers take the fences, and how they hone for elbow room. It would put you out of debt, Billy, and give you a little stake besides, that you could take and. . . ."

"Take and what?"

"Oh . . . I don't know. . . . But, see how everything has broken against you, one thing after another, along with the drought. This 'blossom like the rose' business is all right, but when you have a chance to sell on good terms. . . ."

He knew she was quoting his father in that 'blossom like the rose' stuff. All his life Billy Dwight had heard his father use that foolish old phrase with a humor that was on the surface only. Old Dwight had always dreamed of the day when irrigation would turn their semi-desert range into damp mother-of-gold.

It was four years now since Dwight had known that he would never hear his father use that phrase again. He had never used it much himself, but it seemed to him, even yet, that the dry, punished land was part of the fiber of his bones.

"Irrigation will come someday," Jane was saying in her low, almost husky voice. "The terrain points it, that we know. But we'll never see it, Billy my boy, not us. Better to let Dad have the dry ninety sections, and forget it, once and for all. . . ." Her voice trailed off. For a moment she feared he would think that she was chiseling on behalf of her father, who had land enough, but she decided that, if Billy Dwight didn't know her better than that, then he would never know her at all. "It just seems," she said, "the way everything has gone against you. . . ."

He said unexpectedly: "Well . . . you haven't gone against me yet. Or . . . or have you, maybe?"

She was silent.

"Answer me."

"I . . . I don't know exactly what we're coming to," she said uncertainly.

"Yes, you do."

She glanced at him sidelong, suddenly half afraid of him. He was looking at her steadily, and his eyes seemed to be saying to her: *Now. Now is the time. You can take me now, or take me later, but if it isn't now, it will never be quite the same again.* She thought a woman was cheap who waited to see if her lover was a success or not before making up her mind. A woman who was not willing to work in the harness with the man through the hard years didn't know what loving was, and never would. She didn't want him to think she was one of those. And yet, she didn't know how to tell what was in her mind. She turned in her saddle and met his eyes squarely. "I . . . I. . . ." But once more her eyes dropped, and she turned away.

In that moment he had read her eyes better than she knew. Also, he knew that it was old Tombstone who stood between them now. He had heard from Jane herself the story of what made it possible for the old man to hold his daughter so.

Nearly twenty years before — Jane was twenty now — the Apaches had swarmed over that country in what was to be their last great war. Out of old Mexico, from their inaccessible strongholds in the high Sierra Madres, those last unbroken savages had trailed northward in mounted war parties that raided, burned, and killed, then flicked away like dust wraiths to lose themselves in the desert again.

For months on end the scattered ranchers decamped from their cabins each night and slept in the sage. A cabin was all right during the day, when you could see ten miles, but at night it was a give-away.

Just at that time Jane's mother died. The Apaches were only indirectly to blame for that, for she died of pneumonia, which Tombstone did not know how to fight. Jane was one month old.

Every night at sunset, during those long black weeks, Tombstone had faded off into the sage, his motherless baby in his arms. He had raised her clumsily, but as best he could. From time to time, as his daughter grew older, he had hired different women to keep house for him, but it was Tombstone himself who had been the nearest thing to a mother that the girl ever had.

Now, this Tombstone was a hard man, a tough, fighting type, born so and finished in a hard school. If he had gumption, and high standards of gumption, there was plenty of reason for that. But on his daughter Tombstone had lavished a tenderness of affection never suspected by the outer world. While she had been East at school, his surliness and unrepentant outbursts of savagery had so darkened the local skies that even the cattle, it was said, had tried to climb out of

155

the range, and Tombstone had bitten them individually on the necks as he yanked them unceremoniously back.

Thus it happened that Jane's father was something more to her than a habit and a source of income. When she thought of revolt against his domination, she always recalled some absurd, beloved picture out of her childhood, such as Tombstone's trying to sew doll clothes for her with his gnarled hands, or Tombstone's making faces at her as he fed her with a spoon.

Dwight was taunted by the thought that but for Tombstone this girl was his. "Look at me!" he commanded her.

She tentatively obeyed.

He grinned, and there was an electric vibration to his eye. "You're mine, honey, and don't you forget it!"

"Horse feathers," she said without conviction.

Still, grinning, he leaned in his saddle to hook a long arm about her. For a moment she seemed to lean against his shoulder, then suddenly her horse shot ahead at the dig of her spurs.

Billy Dwight's face tightened with a furious, unaccustomed emotion; he leaned forward, lifting his elbows, and his own pony went after hers in long bounds. He overtook the girl's pony like a cyclone at a hundred yards, and, letting his long reins swing free from the horn, he leaned out of his saddle to lift the girl from her horse as they ran. He clamped her close against him, turned her face upward with one hand, and kissed her mouth.

His decent old pony came to a bounding stop, obviously under the impression that they were doing rope work. Jane wriggled, and her hard, little fist cracked into Dwight's ribs, knocking a grunt out of him.

"I'll bust you loose from your boots!" she hissed. She freed herself and dropped to the ground. Her gray eyes shot sparks. "I don't know as that was so good," she told him. "Bill Dwight, you go catch that paint!"

Obediently he went after the pinto pony, caught it, and came loping back. Jane was sitting on a boulder, shaking out her wind-tangled hair with her fingers. She looked very small and disconsolate to the mounted man. No, he thought, perhaps that hadn't been so good. But his eyes were still smoldering as he handed over her horse.

"Don't you look tough at me, Bill Dwight," she warned him. "You're not such a big shot!"

"I'm gettin' tired of bein' stood up against," he remarked. "Somethin's goin' to

157

get me mad one of these times."

She laughed, half hysterically, and turned her pony's nose toward the Bar Hook, the ranch that Tombstone had made with so little except his daughter in mind, all those twenty years. This time, Dwight did not follow her. At a hundred yards she stopped her horse; he was still motionless in his saddle, watching her go. Jane rode halfway back.

"Listen, Billy. . . ." Her face was sober, but he couldn't tell at that distance whether the emotion in her eyes was sympathy, or pity, or something else. He wanted neither of the former, that was sure. "Listen. If Dad offers you a good price this time, take him like a shot . . . won't you?" There was appeal in her voice.

"One of these times," he called back.

Her pony wheeled, and jumped from the cut of her quirt.

Old Tombstone was still waiting at Dwight's door as the youngster swung down. The old rancher stood up and growled at the man he had come to see.

"I been waiting upwards of an hour," Tombstone informed him.

"Have a good rest?" asked Dwight.

Tombstone's steely eyes gimleted out

from under his shaggy brows, estimating Dwight once more. They were always estimating something, and always arriving at an unfavorable total, to judge by the dourly mustached old face.

"Puttering around," grunted Tombstone, "always puttering around."

"Were you?" said Dwight politely.

Tombstone emitted a sound between a cough and a snarl. He started to resume his seat.

"Have a chair," said Dwight.

Tombstone straightened up as if there had been cactus on the chair. "I've set around this place for one morning," he replied.

Dwight sighed and himself sat down in the seat Tombstone had occupied.

"I come here to make you another offer on this sand patch," Tombstone said bluntly, and Dwight noticed again that the old man knew how to look like the Rock of Gibraltar.

"How much?"

Tombstone named a figure. It was high, more than the land was worth now — even as a speculation. Any figure was high that would leave any money after the debts were lifted. This price would.

"That's the same as you offered before."

The old man snorted. "My offer stands. A

good price now. Five thousand less to-morrow."

Billy Dwight stirred, whistling softly and tunelessly through his teeth. His eyes were on the broken mesas, like a far, buttressed wall. He wondered how much of Tombstone's opposition was based upon a desire for the Dwight lands, and resentment at his inability to buy them even at a price too high. He also wondered if part of Jane's resistance to him was not based on the hatred she expressed for the desert barrens, and her distrust of a life in company with a man tied to his land. For a moment his everlasting optimism offered him a picture of desirability and hope — Tombstone placated; debts wiped out forever; money in his pocket, a footloose freedom, and Jane. But when he opened his mouth, it was to say absentmindedly: "You'll see this yar desert blossom like the rose. . . ."

Tombstone started. "What's that?" He had the sudden impulse that old Dwight himself had spoken.

Billy Dwight ignored him.

Goin' to make a two-mile pancake,
A forty-section, foot-thick pancake,
And spread it on the ground,
And this yar sun will cook that pancake,

**Our lovin' two-mile pancake,
And make it nice and brown.**

Tombstone took a long step to Dwight's side, his eyes spitting hot cinders. "You . . . answer me!" he commanded in a steel-cold, lethal voice that had once been able to clear a saloon, or fill a jail.

"Me?"

"You!"

"Well. . . ." Dwight rolled a cigarette with one hand, spoiled it, started another with two hands, and licked it shut. Over the brown twisted paper he regarded Tombstone without perturbation. "Well . . . we'll see how this drive comes out. . . ."

"The five thousand drop don't include the cattle you lose and spoil," Tombstone pointed out. "You'll have somethin' less than nothin' left, feller, you keep on!"

"Well . . . we'll see. . . ."

That night, Tombstone gave Jane a sketchy but vigorous idea of his opinions ongumption, as distinct from bullheadedness. "That spineless little ninny of a Dwight. . . ."

"Little, Dad?" Billy Dwight was an inch taller than Tombstone.

"I re-far," said her father with dignity, "to

his capabilities and *cay*pacities."

"Oh."

"This rope-backed, kettle-headed jig-a-ree," Tombstone went on, "begun by holdin' more cattle than the range will stand. Dissatisfied with moderate success, he increases 'em after the first drought. Dissatisfied with distinguished setbacks thus brung on hisself, he goes to work and slaps on a mortgage to plant alfalfy, which same not bein' liable to grow without rain comes in anyways two inches high, tharby loses him pants and shirt. Dissatisfied to rest on his florals, him bein' already well on the way to nationwide recognition, and the Congressional Medal for Prime Chump in the boy class, this yar father's own goes to work. . . ."

"Dad . . . I know all that."

"This brings us," Tombstone bore down inexorably, "to present date, havin' waited upwards of a hour, one of our leadin' citizens name of Old Man Mackinson, better known as Tombstone, rides up and. . . ."

"Waits an hour and rides up, Dad!"

"Rides up, I said. Kin a father git a word in edgeways in his own house? Rides up and offers him a price that would be plumb foolish, if it wasn't ridic'lous, to take the whole passel of trouble and free-runnin' misfortune off his hands. All right. Maybeso

162

you picture this weak-kneed grasshopper fallin' on his knees and praisin' Goddelmighty for unhoped-for rescue. Maybe you figure he busts out in hymns o' thanksgivin' that this Tombstone is a soft-headed old pelican, which same is the only kind would offer any such price. Maybe. But guess what he says?"

"What?"

Tombstone warbled fatuously through his nose. "Goin' to spread a pancake! Gonna make a pancake!"

"Dad! You tell me what he said!"

"That's what he said. Listen here, daughter. . . ." Tombstone suddenly dropped his oratory and leaned toward Jane. His eyes were indomitable, but their hardness was underlaid by the tenderness that only his daughter ever aroused. "Listen here, honey . . . what you think of a . . . of a . . . a feller like that?"

"I think," said Jane, "that if a man showed gumption in this world. . . ."

Tombstone exploded. "Gumption! Gumption! It's plain, ordinary bullheaded-ness."

Jane tried to rise inconspicuously. She wanted to be away from there. For three years, off and on, the drought had laid a haunting, nervous tension on that country;

she, least of anyone, was ready for bombardment now.

Tombstone stopped her, and his voice had suddenly changed. She saw that something else was coming, something that she hadn't expected. "Wait, honey. I got somethin' of yours here." He took a match out of his pocket and from it unrolled a long brown hair. "You left this on this . . . this Dwight's brush jacket."

Slowly Jane sat down. "Well?"

"You know what I think of the Dwights, honey?"

"Yes."

"You know what I think of this Dwight?"

Jane smiled wanly. "I guess you've given me a kind of inklin', Dad, from time to time."

"You know where his lack of gumption has brought him?"

"Maybe it wasn't. . . ."

Tombstone snapped savagely: "Lack of gumption, I said!"

"All right, Dad."

Tombstone's steel eyes softened a little. The girl took after her mother, which meant, after all, that the Mackinson gumption was likely to end with him in his grave. "You know he's staking his last chance in this drive?"

"I know that, Dad."

"You know that drive can't help but lose everything there is in it?"

Instinctively she turned to her father to know what was truth and what was fantasy, even in this affair in which Tombstone himself was such a rock-ribbed factor. "Dad! Tell me the truth!"

"Did I ever tell you anything else, honey?"

"Has Billy Dwight a chance to pull out of the hole?"

"Honey, not one in a million!"

Jane wilted. But it was not Dwight's financial fortune she was interested in — although that meant enough, too. It was that, if Billy could have pulled himself through, then perhaps Tombstone could have looked at him differently, after all. She wasn't ready yet to break the heart of that stern old man, who twenty years before had carried her through the mesquite in one arm, his long gun in the crook of the other. Suddenly the tears appeared in her eyes. "Dad, let me go away."

"Go? Where?"

"Anywhere! I hate this country, every patch of cactus in it, every blade of grass!"

Tombstone looked a hundred years old. Women were funny. The range would be empty and meaningless when she was gone;

but she'd be back; at least, he guessed she would. "All right, honey. You can go, if you want."

During the succeeding month a shadow lay heavily on the Bar Hook, with Jane listless, and Tombstone silent and depressed. From time to time word came to them of the ghastly losses of the small cattlemen whose dwindled herds made up the pool of cattle that died like flies in the dust of the march, dropping blunt-nosed into the dust, and never getting up. Only a pitiful remnant ever reached the distant range for which they had set out, and there the last of the herds found forage only little better than they had left behind. All the Southwest suffered that year, in the grip of the long drought, for the winter had been without snow in the uplands, and the desert was dust.

It was all over at last. One day when Tombstone came in, he said: "Well, he's home."

Her question — "Who?" — was without meaning, and in reply he only mumbled: "Who'd'ja suppose?"

"Has he anything left?"

"Uhn-uh. Well, debts, and an equity in the Dwight range."

"Seems you were right, Dad."

"Uhn-huh. Got any message for him?"

"You goin' over there?"

"Sure I am," said Tombstone. "I got the papers all made out. He'll sell now, all right, and I won't be losin' so much on it." Under his recent somberness she perceived a thin, cold gleam of something like elation, something he got out of seeing one more protagonist of no gumption arrive at his just desserts to Tombstone's profit.

"Tell him," she said, "I'm sorry it came out the way it did."

". . . way it done," Tombstone corrected.

"All right."

He found old Dwight's youngster looking slimmer than ever and considerably more sober, yet Billy Dwight was able to summon up a sort of eye twinkle and a grin, when he saw Tombstone swing down. In his moment of victory Tombstone was prepared to be quite friendly with Billy Dwight.

"Well, I guess you'll be pullin' stakes for some place farther on," Tombstone suggested, not unkindly.

"I guess so, Tombstone. Maybe."

"My daughter," offered Tombstone conversationally, "she's goin' away. Visitin' Cousin Sal for a while."

Dwight's interest quickened. "When's she coming back?"

Tombstone experienced one of the rare let-downs in which he let his own grievances be glimpsed. "Sometimes," he said carelessly, "I think she ain't."

"She ain't?" Billy repeated.

Tombstone recovered himself. "I got the contract o' sale made out. I guess you'll leave me take the sand patch off your hands now."

"I guess so," Dwight conceded.

"You know my price."

"Yep, I know your price."

For the moment the panic that had swept Dwight at word of Jane's indefinite absence was succeeded by a rush of gratitude to the hard, old man. After all, Tombstone's very tenacity of purpose now constituted Billy Dwight's ace in the hole. There would be little left over, when the debts were paid, but he would be footloose and free, with the world ahead of him. He could go seek out the girl who meant more to him than breathing, and Tombstone would be placated at last.

"Come in and set," he said, leading the way to his deal table. "Let's see how the contract reads."

"Ain't much to read. Here's where you

sign. Nosey Tolley, he'll witness, I guess."

Billy Dwight took up his pen, dipped it in the ink. *Here goes nothing,* he was thinking to himself. He glanced up and saw something almost like pity in Tombstone's eyes, looked down and read the contract again, raised the pen, and slammed it, in a splatter of ink, against the opposite wall.

"No!" he exploded.

Tombstone's head jerked up. "You fool . . . you don't mean you won't sell *now?*"

"No, by God! Not now, nor next year, nor the year after that!"

"That price is. . . ."

"Not at any price! Nor at any time, nor to any man."

"You'll never make a go, hangin' on like a. . . ."

"The hell I won't! What do you know about it?" He got up abruptly.

Tombstone rose to face him, the dark blood coming up into his hardened, leather face. An enormous, bulldozing fury was in the old man. "You spineless ninny!" he roared. "You rope-backed, rattle-headed, jackass kid, by God, you'll squirm. . . ."

Dwight shot out a lean jaw. "Shut up!" he shouted.

Tombstone's voice stopped. He hadn't

been shouted at in many a long year. "Why, you. . . ."

"I'll tell you what you're going to do," said Dwight, his voice lower now, but so hard that it cut Tombstone's down. "You're going to take yourself by the seat of the pants and hoist yourself onto that horse, then you're going to take that horse by the seat of *his* pants and hoist him on home."

Tombstone stared. After all, the man before him was only a kid. He shrugged. "Well . . . it's your ranch," he admitted, as he turned away.

"You're damned tootin'."

Dwight was grinning now, but without the apologetic note that had always characterized old Dwight. "Come back, when you're feelin' better sometime, and maybe, if you live, you'll see this yar desert blossom like the rose."

Jane couldn't read the faintly dazed expression of her father when he again swung down at the gates of the Bar Hook.

"Did he say anything about . . . did he . . . ?" Her voice trailed off.

"Very little," said Tombstone. "But I reckon it was enough. He told me to get the hell off his place."

"Dad. In those words?"

"His exact words . . ." — Tombstone hesitated — "was to the general and pointed effect," he finished lamely.

"Then . . . he didn't *sell?*"

"No, he didn't sell."

"He won't sell *now?*"

"Are you deaf? He says not now, not next year, no time, no price, no man. The little fool figgers to make a stick of it, I guess. The little rope-backed, rattle-headed. . . ." He paused, checked by the change in his daughter's face. Tombstone thought himself a genteel sort of feller, such as never swore at his daughter, if it could be got around, but he was surprised into something very close to it now. "What the devil *you* fixin' to fight?"

"*You,*" said Jane bluntly.

"Who, *me?*"

"Get this. I don't buck you very often, but I'm buckin' you now. Billy Dwight has more gumption than anybody but a Mackinson ever thought of, you hear? If he's going to fight it out on this busted-up lay-out, I'm going to stick it with him, and I'd like to see anybody stop me, Mackinson or Dwight. Give me that horse."

Her quick hand shortened the stirrup leathers to their fourth notch.

"You're *what?*" Tombstone got out.

"You heard me all right," said Tombstone's daughter. "You think you've got a corner on all the gumption there is?"

"Where you goin'? Get off that horse!"

"I'm going to tell Billy Dwight to get some clean sheets in."

"Jane!"

She skittered the horse sideways out of reach, and Tombstone was forced to halt and try parley. "I thought . . . I thought you said you hated this country."

"I love every patch of cactus and every blade of grass in it," said Jane fervently. "Anyway . . . you're going to see the desert bloom. . . ."

"Shut up!" roared Tombstone. "I've stood enough!"

When she had galloped out of earshot, Tombstone ran for the corral, eared down a raw broncho to the snubbing post, and eased a saddle on. Then he slowed up, freed the pony's head, kicked it in the stomach, and left it trying to climb the fence, saddle and all. He went to sit on his doorstep alone.

"I don't know," said Tombstone to himself, "but what, after all, gumption may be picking up. . . . Well," he sighed wearily, for his bones were old, "so it goes. . . ."

STAR ON HIS HEART

Cap Trainor realized he was getting old. He grasped the saddle horn hard as his beautiful sorrel gelding trotted along the trail. A thin cloud of dust hung motionless behind him, for not a breath of air was stirring. The sun was an hour high, but the prairie was cold and gray, and the east was hidden by a dark cloudbank that remained like a curtain halfway to the zenith.

The ride was in the line of duty, and it was the only one left to Cap Trainor from his long years of service as sheriff of the turbulent Sheridan County. He eased himself in the saddle, for an old wound in his side was aching, and a pain stabbed him in the back. He had not come unscathed through his years as a lawman.

Old he might be, yet his keen blue-gray eyes peered far across the prairie, and he counted twenty-seven cattle moving single file along a path to a water hole. An old song that had been written by some unknown range troubadour was running through his head, and he began singing it softly. He thrilled with the thought that it might have been written about him.

**Don't go foolin' with an old lawman,
For he's lightnin' on the draw . . .**

He wondered if that were still true of him. An old man, with the pain of wounds that had long healed, would hardly be the one to draw and fire a gun in split-second time. Many months had passed since Cap Trainor had used a gun, and he wondered if his hand had lost any of its speed and accuracy.

An hour later he rode into Buckskin, a small town with frame buildings on each side of a wide main street. A brick bank building stood on a corner. Across the street was a frame hotel that did a thriving business every Saturday night. Occasionally a traveling man stopped there and brought news from an outside world.

Cap tied his horse to a hitch rack. Stiffly he strode along the board sidewalk. Three men came out of a saloon, and Cap stopped as they came up to him. One was wearing a sheriff's badge. He was a powerful, beetle-browed man, and he stared at Trainor as though surprised.

His two companions stood beside him, as

though they were ready to back his play, whatever that might be.

"Howdy, Trainor," the sheriff said. "I thought you was hidin' out on that little spread o' yourn, kinda ashamed-like. Are you still sore about the lickin' you got at the last election?"

A sharp retort sprang to the old man's lips, but he choked it back. A hot temper had been his greatest weakness in the old days. When he spoke, his voice was serene and gentle. "No, Hatch, I never was sore about being defeated. I know I was getting too old for the job, but I did hope. . . ." He paused.

"What did you hope?"

"I hoped to have someone take over who. . . ." Again he paused.

Hatch sneered, and there was an ugly expression on his coarse face. "What are you drivin' at, you ol' has-been?"

"Nothing," he answered. "I'd been wantin' to retire for ten years."

He turned away, but Hatch stepped forward, leering. His two gunmen were close behind. Slim Wilson opened his thin lips in a smile that disclosed a toothless upper jaw. Bull Marvin stood with folded arms, his face stoical and expressionless. Cap Trainor knew that Bull was fast.

Hatch seemed bent on following up the conversation. "You started to say somethin' about me!" he ejaculated. "Go ahead an' say it. If you got anything ag'in' me, spit it out."

Trainor faced him, and there was a slight flush coloring his cheeks. "Someday there may be an investigation of that election, Hatch," he said, and his voice had the quality of icicles striking together. "You beat me by seven votes, an' that's mighty close in any man's county. In Blaine township the election board counted me two votes. I've met fourteen men from over there who are ready to swear they voted for me."

Clem Hatch's face flushed. He took a step forward, and his fists clenched. "Do you mean to say the election was crooked?" he snarled.

Before Trainor could answer, a man stepped out of the saloon door and joined them. He was of slender build, and his movements had the lithe quickness of a tiger. He wore a long black coat, a broad-brimmed black hat, and a close-cropped mustache. Both his dress and his soft, white hands disclosed the professional gambler.

"What is the trouble, Clem?" he asked quietly.

"This here old wreck says the election was crooked."

The man smiled. "Is it possible there could be anything but honesty and honor in the county where Cap Trainor was still sheriff?" he asked pleasantly. "If so, all of us will be glad to help find the guilty parties. Isn't that so, men?"

"It sure is, Flash." Slim grinned.

Flash shot a meaningful glance at the glowering Clem Hatch, who grumbled under his breath but said no more.

Cap Trainor continued on his way along the boardwalk. Of all the people he knew, the beetle-browed new sheriff was the only one who could arouse his anger. In the grim school of experience he had learned to be as unemotional as the law itself. There was no place left in his heart for personal feeling. Hard and impersonal he had become through the long years, as hard and impersonal as the bone-handled .45 that used to swing at his side.

Yet Cap Trainor knew that he was neither hard nor cold, and it was on an errand of mercy that he had come today. He went into a general store, and made his way past counters piled high with clothing, hardware, groceries, saddles, and even medicine. He paused by a young man who was stacking boxes of shoes on the shelves. "Howdy, Harry," he greeted.

The young man turned. "I was comin' out tonight, Sheriff," he began hastily. "Really I was. I. . . ."

"That's all right, son. I just came in to save you the trouble. You're all the responsibility I got now, an' I really like to ride in an' see you."

The young man began coughing, and leaned against the counter. He touched his lips with a handkerchief.

Cap Trainor frowned. "How are you feelin', Harry?" he asked quietly.

"Oh, I ain't so bad. Doc Sanders says, if I could go to a sanitarium in Denver a few months, I might get all right again. But I got this job, Sheriff, an' I'll stick it out."

Cap regarded his charge with keen eyes. It was plain that the boy was in no condition to work. In fact, Trainor had suspected from the first that Harry had been let out on parole because they didn't want him to die in the penitentiary. Placing him under the charge of Cap Trainor, who was then sheriff, was a mere formality. Harry was to report to him each month, and this was the day for his appearance.

"Someday, Harry," Cap began in a low voice, "you'll tell me who really stuck up the Brigham bank, an' who killed the cashier."

Harry looked down at the floor. His lips

set in a stubborn line. "I don't know nothin' about it," he said.

"You been sayin' that a long time, son, an' so far it's got you exactly no place. A year an' a half in the pen, a touch o' t.b., an' I don't know what all. I ain't askin' you what the real reason is, son, but someday you'll tell me all about it. That's the best way. I'll go now, an' I'll send in a report to the warden that you're workin' an' doin' fine."

"Thanks, Sheriff."

Cap walked away, then turned, and came back. "What's Clem Hatch an' his gunnies doin' here in Buckskin?" he asked.

A startled expression came into Harry's eyes. "I don't know, Sheriff. I didn't know they was in town."

It was plain that he was telling the truth.

"Keep away from that outfit, Harry. They're pizon. They got you in bad before, an' they'll do it again. Flush Ranson is here, too." He looked keenly at Harry's face as he spoke.

"Yeah, I know. He bought the saloon last week. He's all right, Sheriff. Flash isn't a bad man."

"Mebbe so. I hear two men held up the stage at the foot of Caljas Pass. That's the first one in nearly four years."

Harry looked up defiantly. "Flush didn't

179

have nothin' to do with it. He ain't a bandit."

Again Trainor turned away. The stage robbery was not the only thing that had happened, but it was no business of his. He made a few purchases, and an hour later his sorrel gelding was trotting steadily along the trail.

Ahead, lost in the blue-gray haze, was the little ranch where he had retired after his defeat. He had owned it ten years, and he hoped to die there; soon, he thought, for he was old and weary and discouraged, and a sharp pain was stabbing him in the back.

His heart went out to Harry who was frail and sick and under the cloud of a prison sentence. There was something peculiar about the whole thing. Cap always had felt that Harry was innocent. The boy was neither robber nor murderer. He was a comparative stranger, and Cap thought he acted as though he were shouldering the crime for another. The boy should go to a sanitarium until he was well. Cap would have given him the money, if he had had it, but the old man needed capital badly. His little ranch would keep him if he could stock it with cattle. Now he was getting only a small rental for the range land and hay. As long as he was sheriff, there was a chance of picking up a reward in addition to the salary.

It was nearly noon when he reached home. Turning the gelding into the corral, he went into the tiny house. Everything was neat and clean, but with the severity and plainness found in the home of the bachelor. He prepared a simple meal, washed the dishes, and tidied up the kitchen. Wearily he walked out to the corral and stood with arms resting on the top plank. He pictured it full of white-face steers bearing his brand. In imagination he could see cattle on the range, fattening on the rich buffalo and grama grass. He would like to have a hundred cows, and the increase would mean an old age of plenty in three or four years when the fat, grass-fed steers reached the market in Kansas City or even Chicago. He shook his head wearily. It was not for him. He must struggle along as best he could, for cattle required money, and money Cap Trainor did not have.

He was roused from his dreams by the drumming of hoofs. Someone was coming up the trail. The rider drew up in a cloud of dust, and jumped from the lathering, blowing horse.

It was Harry. "Sheriff," he gasped out in a fit of coughing, "you gotta help me! They framed me before, an' they're framin' me again. You're the only friend I got, Sheriff, an' you can't let 'em get away with it."

"Now, son," came the steady, calm voice of the old man, "just take it easy. What's it all about? Start at the beginnin'."

Harry leaned weakly against the corral. "He wasn't bad," he babbled. "He just sort of wanted power an' money. He wasn't a bad man at all. It was Clem Hatch an' the others. He thought Clem would work for him, an' he kept 'em from doin' all the things they wanted to. That's why they killed him."

"Killed who?"

"Flush. Flush Ranson."

"When was he killed?"

"This noon. I left the store to go to lunch."

"Who killed him?"

"Clem Hatch, an' now they've framed me for it, an' they think they'll get me like they did before. But I'll show 'em. I'll tell the whole thing. I'll even. . . ."

Cap Trainor's voice interrupted, and it was the cold, hard voice of the old lawman: "Tell me just what happened."

"I stopped in the saloon to . . . to see Flash. He was there alone at that time. Just as I went in, Clem Hatch rose up from behind the bar and shot Flash in the back. He'd never dare to shoot it out with

Flush, face to face."

"Go on. What happened?"

"Slim an' Bull jumped out from behind the bar where they'd been hidin', an' grabbed me. They always back up Clem's dirty play. They said I killed Flush, an' they'd caught me dead to rights."

"Did they know you was comin' in at that time?"

"Flush knew, an' he may have told 'em. I don't know. Anyway, I walked in just at the right time to get framed."

"How did you get away?"

"First they said they was goin' to hang me. Then they said to get out of town as fast as I could. I started away, an' they all began shootin' at me. If I hadn't stumbled, the first shot would have got me in the back of the head."

"I see. Then you grabbed a horse from the hitch rack, an' got away."

"Yeah, that's right. They'll be after me, but they won't know I came here."

"Son," said Cap gently, "they'll pick up a couple o' cowboys that know how to trail, an' they'll follow you across the prairie for a thousand miles. You can't get away."

"But why did they try to kill me after tellin' me to get out?"

Cap frowned. "It's because a fool county

183

board offers a bigger reward for a man dead than alive. Son, you was bein' shot while tryin' to escape. It's an old custom in some places."

He stood with wrinkled brow. A mile away was a thin cloud of dust, and he made out a number of horses and riders. Clem Hatch and his men were on the trail.

"That's the whole trouble, son," he said grimly. "You'll be shot while tryin' to escape. Then you can't tell your story, an' Clem will collect a three-thousand-dollar reward for bringin' in a killer."

"Then I gotta get away, Sheriff." Harry sagged weakly against the corral and coughed. The excitement and hard ride had been too much for him. "Can you give me a fresh horse? It's three against one, an' I ain't got a friend in the world."

"Yes, you have, son. But fresh horse or not, you can't get away. Don't you think it's time to come clean? What was you doin' around Flush?"

"There ain't any use keepin' mum any more, Sheriff. I was tryin' to get him to go right. I promised my mother, you see."

"Your mother? What did she have to do with it?"

"She married him after my father died. Until Flush left, he was mighty good to her, an' he was mighty good to me, too. He was my stepdad, an' was a regular prince."

"I see. So you went to the pen to cover up for him."

"I thought so, but now I know he didn't have nothin' to do with it. You see it was ten years ago when he left, an' he didn't know who I was till yesterday."

"Who held up the bank and killed the cashier?"

"Clem Hatch an' Bull Marvin."

Cap Trainor's frown deepened. "It's too bad you didn't talk at the trial, son. It would have saved a lot of trouble. You can see that now."

The posse had turned from the main trail and was headed straight for Cap's ranch. The old man set his jaw hard, and took down a rope that was hanging over a post. Grimly he coiled it. Suddenly the loop shot out, settled over Harry's head and arms. Five seconds later the boy lay hog-tied and helpless.

"I'm takin' you in, son," Trainor said gruffly. "Mebbe you didn't do the killin', but it's up to me to find out. You're on parole to me, an' I'm responsible for what you do. An', besides, there ain't goin' to be no killin' while tryin' to escape."

Harry burst into tears. "I thought you was

my friend," he sobbed. "But I guess there ain't no such thing."

Six men rode up. Three were C-in-a-Box cowboys who had been following the trail. The others were Clem Hatch and his two gunmen.

"Howdy," Cap greeted. "If you're after somebody charged with killin' Flush Ranson, I've got him all tied up an' waiting' for the hangman. There's a standin' reward in this country for killers, you know, an' I need money bad."

Hatch grinned. "Yeah, that's right, Trainor. It's two thousand cold cash if you bring 'em in alive, an' three thousand if you bring 'em in dead. I believe you always turned 'em over dead when you was sheriff."

Cap winced. "I collected on one." It was not a pleasant memory. He had protested when the county board passed the reward resolution, telling them it meant the killing of innocent men. His protest was ignored, for feeling was running high over the murder of a prominent cattleman.

The cowboys regarded Harry curiously. They had done the tracking as a lark, for they were on their way home when Hatch took them into his posse. Without a word to Cap, they turned their horses and continued on their way. The sheriff and his men dismounted.

"It's nice of you to have him all ready for us, Trainor," Hatch said.

"I didn't have him all ready for you," Cap answered. "He was paroled to me, an' I'm takin' him in myself."

"No need o' that. We came out just to get him."

"Yeah, I know all about it, Hatch. But you see I need money bad, an' I'm hangin' onto my prisoner. I ain't even turnin' him over to any sheriff. I'm takin' him straight to the county jail at Central City. I been waitin' for a break like this ever since I went out of office."

"So the great Cap Trainor ain't above makin' a little money on the side," Hatch sneered. "No hurry about it, though. We'll rest the horses a bit, an' mebbe you an' me is due for a little gab fest."

It was mid-afternoon. Hatch and his men squatted close together in the shade of the corral and carried on a low-voiced conversation. Harry lay without moving, his eyes closed.

Cap leaned over him. "Is the rope too tight, son?" he asked.

Harry turned his head away and did not answer. Cap began loosening the bonds.

"Leave him be," Hatch snarled. "We don't want any getaway, at least not now."

Cap looked at him curiously. Hatch was showing his true colors. Lawman he might be from the result of a crooked election, but never could he be other than bandit and killer.

"I get you, Hatch," Cap said slowly. "I know what you mean when you say that . . . 'at least not now.' Only this time you ain't givin' orders to your yellow-livered gunmen."

"No, I'm givin' orders to an ol' man who used to be the sheriff," Hatch sneered.

"An' do you think I'll carry out your orders?"

"Yeah, for two reasons. First, I'm the sheriff, an', second, I got a gun and you ain't."

Cap did not answer. The belt and gun that he had worn at his side so many years was hanging in the kitchen.

Hatch rose to his feet. "Listen, you ol', worn-out has-been," he snarled. "We're takin' this killer back to town. You ain't goin' with us, an' you ain't gettin' my cut in the reward. Is that plain?"

Slim Benton and Bull Marvin moved up and stood just behind Hatch. Slim was grinning. Cap looked from one to the other.

"Are you backin' Hatch's play?" he asked.

"We sure are," Slim answered. "A thousand smackers each ain't bad money for one day."

Cap stooped slightly. As if by magic a six-gun appeared in his hand. It had come from a shoulder holster that he had worn every day for more than thirty years. "Reach high!" he commanded tersely. "I'm takin' over."

Hatch's eyes were hard. He lifted his hands slightly, palms forward. "So you're resistin' the law, are you, Trainor?"

"No, I ain't resistin' the law. I'm defendin' the law. To do it, I'm turnin' over a gang of killers. I know all about it, Hatch. I know how you framed this boy for both killin's. An' I knew you'd be after him, an' that he'd be shot while tryin' to escape. I couldn't do a thing with the three cowboys you had trackin', for they wouldn't understand and would stick with the law. That's why I tied up the boy before you came. You couldn't shoot a helpless prisoner. He didn't understand, but I had to make the whole thing look real."

Harry opened his eyes, and now he looked at Cap with amazement. "Golly, Sheriff," he muttered, "I sure had you wrong."

Hatch stood without moving, his men at

his back. Bull Marvin edged slightly behind the sheriff. Suddenly his hand dropped to his gun.

There was a spout of flame as Cap fired. A round hole appeared in Bull's low forehead, and he fell forward.

Hatch dropped to one knee, drawing his weapon as he moved. Slim jumped sideways to the left, and it was at him that Cap fired. The bullet caught Slim in the arm. He turned completely around, and stood staring at a red hand that hung limply.

Cap sprang to one side as he shot. Hatch, on one knee, jerked a bullet and then another, but the old man moved so fast that both shots missed. Again Cap's gun roared. Hatch remained a moment with gun held out. His jaw dropped, the weapon fell to the ground, and he slumped forward on his face.

Harry rose to his feet. His face was white, but he smiled. "That was pretty slick the way you loosened the rope, Sheriff. If I could have got untied a moment sooner, I'd have got Hatch. Bull's gun fell right by me."

Cap was looking at Slim. "I want you to talk, Slim," he said. "An' see that you talk fast an' straight. You may save your neck by doin' it."

Slim talked. Hatch had done the killings,

and Slim would tell his story in court. Cap bound up the man's wound.

An hour later a small procession filed along the main street of Buckskin. Slim Benton came first, his arm in a sling. Behind him came Harry. Two horses were next with the bodies of Hatch and Bull slung across the saddles. Cap Trainor, hard-eyed, stoical, followed behind them all.

He turned the bodies over to Peter Varney, the coroner, and said in a low voice: "See that Harry gets the reward, Pete. The boy needs it for a term at a sanitarium. Doc says he ain't very bad, an' he'll come out all well an' fine. He'll have enough money left to start a little business, an' I'll keep on lookin' after him. Put Slim Benton in jail an' keep him there. He has a story to tell that'll interest everyone."

For the second time that day Cap Trainor rode homeward. He was very tired. Old wounds were aching, and a sharp pain was stabbing him in the back. Yet he was happy. Harry would get well. That would pay for some of Hatch's cruelty to the boy. For Cap Trainor, there was his little ranch. The fact that he had no cattle didn't matter. He would get along some way.

He breathed deeply as he looked at the

western sky. It was aflame with a sun that was sinking into the horizon. Above it was a single cloud blazing with red and purple and gold. Cap drank in the scene.

"Somehow," he muttered, "I always think the sun is a lot prettier when it sets than when it rises. I wonder if the same thing is true with men."

Softly he began humming the words of the lawman's song.

**Now don't feel sorry for the old lawman
When he lays down to die,
For a better place is waitin'
When he goes up there on high. . . .**

Cap Trainor was very happy.

THE BATTLE OF
GUNSMOKE LODE

A lead messenger ricocheted a hundred feet before Lon Helms, and went droning over his head. Immediately the *slat-slat* of the echoed report rattled all up and down Crazy Woman's Cañon. That was Elkhorn Sneed, trying the range. Helms waited, planning to shift his position after the third shot, but Sneed held his fire.

Lon Helms continued his leisurely smoking, his rifle on his crossed knees. Below him the cañon widened, but here, fifty feet on either hand, the silver-gray granite walls rose in sheer jagged steps, a hundred feet at a throw, offering no foothold. He had chosen a position on a slide of small rock that filled the gulch to a depth of hundreds of feet and reached downcañon half a mile in a long, naked slope. Therein lay the only advantage on the side of his forlorn-hope defense; even by starlight you could see the figure of a man a thousand yards off against that white granite.

Nor would he be attacked from the rear. Behind him Crazy Woman's Cañon struck but a little deeper into the range, a twisting cleft, and the end was a blind pocket that would have been a trap for mountain sheep. A few years ago there had been a way out, by the Upper Shelf, that led you into the Crush Cañon country, but another of those rock slides, by which the centuries had been whittling away the great Pilot Range, cut that off. That balanced slide now barred the way, striking downward at a desperate angle to hang poised on the lip of Crush Cañon itself. Someday a fly would light on that slide and send the whole business thundering into Crush Cañon.

Helms ran an unhurried gray eye over the broken cover half a mile below. Beyond the foot of the talus a sprinkling of scrub piñon, juniper, and big boulders made it possible for riflemen to get almost to the foot of the slide unseen. He thought, though, that he had most of his besiegers located now.

Bluegum Ides himself, boss of his gang and boss of Little Hat, was over to the left in a pile of rocks. A couple of hundred feet nearer, and almost in the middle of the widened cañon, Terry O'Case lay in a juniper clump. That was like O'Case, to be out in front — a good cowboy, once, that whisky had got.

Elkhorn Sneed, the gray-mustached old reprobate with the uncommonly long-barreled rifle, was way over to the right, and up on a shelf. This was the man Helms had to fear; Sneed would try some fancy shooting from that position, no doubt.

Helms had spotted one other — Big Foot Scott, a black-looking hulk of a man, crippled up from early broncho riding, and now a dirty-job man for Ides. Big Foot was far down the cañon, where he had a built a cooking fire.

Now a fifth figure detached itself from Bluegum Ides's rock pile. It was waving something gray over its head — presumably a shirt that had once been white. Presently this man started up the slide, hands over his head. Helms snapped off the safety of his rifle and half raised it to send down a warning shot, but he changed his mind and let the climbing figure come on.

While he waited for the shirt-waver to toil up the long half mile, Helms let his eyes stray to the mouth of the prospect hole a hundred feet below him in the cañon wall. Only a little black hole like a socket without an eye — but Ides would be glad to kill a man to get hold of it.

The mistake Helms had made was in letting a Little Hat man assay his samples. Little Hat, no more than five ramshackle buildings that gave their name to a mountain-hemmed strip of country, was exclusively run by the shenanigans of Bluegum Ides, and Helms should have known that the semi-professional assayer would prove to be in Bluegum's pay.

Ides was called variously a road agent, claim jumper, border smuggler, and stock rustler, but within his own Little Hat range he did as he chose, and never hesitated to rest his claim in the supreme court of Judge Colt. The gang that backed him was as unprincipled as he was — if such a thing could be.

Five hours after the assay of Lon Helms's ore, Helms had learned that a crack Indian tracker, Mono Logan by name, was back-trailing him, searching the hills for the monuments that marked the strike, and Mono Logan was in the pay of Bluegum Ides. A storekeeper's daughter in Little Hat had brought Helms word of that.

Helms immediately saw that he faced a Chinaman's choice. He could ride hell-for-leather to the county seat, and record his claim — in which case he would return to find that Mono Logan had searched it out, and that Ides had moved his monuments and grabbed the claim as his own, with gunsmoke to prove it up. Or he could back-track, establish a defensible position, and back up his rights with gunfire. This meant that Ides would beat him to the recordation, but he had decided that this was the best he could do.

Instantly he sent word across a desert and a range to the only friend he had whose power exceeded that of Bluegum Ides's, to Jim Morton, chief engineer for the ten-million-dollar Purple Aster Mine. In his message he conveyed to Morton certain explicit directions beginning: **If you can bring a pack train, and half a dozen men that are prepared and willing to fight. . . .** His proposition was to go partners with the Purple Aster.

It was heavy on his mind now that he had little to offer the Purple Aster, even if Jim Morton should come. By this time Ides would have recorded a claim to a site in Crazy Woman's Cañon, and Helms had no more to show than if he had been the claim jumper, instead of Ides. Yet he could not persuade himself to yield. He had water and grub. His grip on the cañon might be meaningless in the end — but it was all he had left of his rights to a discovery that he believed worth millions. One thing — he told himself — remained: the gold was still in the vein.

The climbing figure, approaching into closer range, proved to be no member of the Ides gang, but an old Indian known to Helms by the name of Charley Frog. He came on slowly, occasionally waving his shirt, and half an hour passed before he reached the top, limping in high-heeled boots from which gun wads had been cut to make room for his bunions.

"How?" said Helms.

"Yeah," said Charley Frog. He put on his shirt, belting the tail outside of his Levi pants. "Yeah." The old Indian eased his bowlegged frame to a squat, and twisted a cigarette. "Bluegum says . . . come down now, give you one fifth. Stay up and fight . . . boy, good bye!"

"Tell him to go lay an egg."

"You gone nuts?" asked Charley Frog. "Bluegum, he's beat you to the re-cord."

"You sure he's got it recorded?"

"Gerald Ides hightailed to Underholt this morning, for that one thing. They wait to see what place you head back for, then. Quick re-cord. You make two-ton mistake."

"Yes," admitted Helm. "And if I'd made a run to record it myself, that would have been another. Mono Logan would have back-trailed me to my monuments all right. I'd have got back from Underholt to find my monuments moved two hundred yards downcañon, and Bluegum's outfit high-grading the vein, with twenty men to swear he located a month ago. My word against twenty, and my monuments moved."

"No hope," Charley Frog nodded. "You can't do no business in the Little Hat country, not against Bluegum. You should find some place else, far off."

"The gold," said Helm, "is still in the vein."

Charley Frog surveyed him slowly. He liked this tall, sandy youngster. He recognized that there was a stubbornness in Helms that made talk of no use — big, quiet, leisurely, but as deadly stubborn as a mountain, or a mule. No setting of the jaw was necessary to Helms, for that single-mindedness of his was built into the fiber of the man.

"You sent for friends? Big miners, maybe?" Charley guessed.

"The Purple Aster," Helms told him.

Charley Frog chuckled explosively. "What you got to show the Purple Aster? Pretty quick, Bluegum fills his people in here. Your monuments . . . to hell. Your word against twenty . . . to hell. Your record

. . . ain't any. What you got to show?"

"God knows," said Helms.

"No difference. You be all through, pretty quick. Margie Wilson . . . she likes you . . . but she won't know which rock pile flowers want put. Bluegum says tell you that."

"Tell him," said Helms, for the first time furiously, "flowers want put in his hair. Now get the hell out!"

"Brains gone *bloomp*," Charlie Frog mumbled, leaving.

Half an hour after Charlie Frog's descent the rattling *slam* of Ides's riflery broke out below, reverberating between the cañon walls. That was an expression of opinion, more than anything else, for the light was failing now. Presently Helms climbed a few yards up the slide, to a place where he had scooped out a rifle pit.

By the time he had eaten a can of beans, the sun was deep behind the cañon walls. Beyond the vast vertical rock stands, the darkening sky was saffron, and against it the broken ribs of the world stuck up in silhouette, black and harsh, bristling at the far high crests with myriad small points that would have been trees in another country, but here were jagged splinters of rock. In a notch of the rock barrier a single puddle of deep color glowed as in a cup — purple, blood-red, cobalt, and orange, and its warmth made him think of Margie Williams again.

He shivered, and drew a blanket around his shoulders. Far up behind him, against a blue-black sky, a single gaunt peak shone with the last touch of the sun, as bright as gold-shot quartz — the quartz that was still in the vein. He set himself to wait.

Bluegum was not a man to remain idle long. Moreover, not too much investigation, by the Purple Aster or anyone else, was wanted by Bluegum Ides. Ides held the Little Hat country in a close grip — but Little Hat extended only so far.

Just before midnight Bluegum Ides tried to force the slide. There was no moon, and even against the white granite the visibility within the cañons was very low. Helms first fired at six hundred yards, to let them know that they were seen, and rolled a few fifteen- and twenty-pound rocks down for impressiveness. A bounding rock on a loose slide carries a certain loud authority in semidarkness.

Bluegum Ides and his men fanned out on either side of Helms, approached stubbornly, crawling upward on hands and knees. At two hundred yards Helms spoke to them from his rifle pit: "This is your last warning."

He let go a shot that ricocheted almost in the face of Bluegum himself. The shadowy shapes on the granite flattened themselves, and for a time were still, but presently they shifted and began to fade, and Helms knew that the Ides outfit was moving back down.

Twice more that night Ides led his men up the long white slope of the talus, feeling Helms out, and twice more Helms sent them back.

Dawn came slow and late from behind the thirteen-thousand-foot barrier of the Pilots. When the light was clear, Helms ate again. Then, deliberately, he stretched himself out in this rocky rifle pit, his hat over his face, and went to sleep. Already he had been awake for twenty-four hours. If he was to hold out longer, he must outguess the jumpers. He wondered, as he dozed, if the Purple Aster men were on the way, and what they would be able to do for him — if they chose to do anything — should they come.

All day long Helms roused himself at intervals, but the day proved his judgment sound, for the peace remained undisturbed in Crazy Woman's Cañon. At dusk he rose and stretched at last, thoroughly refreshed.

Hours passed in silent starlight. Ides's watch fire twinkled, a clear spark, far down the cañon, but for a long time Bluegum and his men did not approach. Then, a long time after midnight, Helms became aware that something was moving on the slide. Bluegum and his men were taking their time now. Slowly they crawled up the treacherous footing, pinning themselves flat to the chopped granite, and not a pebble rolled down, not a rock turned under the weight of a knee. Moreover, tonight these men were far less easy to see. Helms guessed they had stripped off their dark outer clothing and crept upward in their underwear, which matched the rock.

They were in single file this time, working their way close under the shadow of the north wall, and they were within a hundred yards before Helms saw them at all. A shock stirred him as he made them out; he had not believed they could come so near.

Helms spoke in a conversational tone: "Ain't you cold, Bluegum, crawling around the mountain in just your lingerie?"

The gray crawling forms froze to immobility, and were still for so long that they might have been shapes of rock. Helms waited them out. He knew what suspense those men were in, depending for their lives upon a discredited invisibility that was their only defense. It was a satisfaction to know that, confused by their long stalk, they could only guess at his general location above. He could have bagged a couple of them, but he didn't want that, since it might mean ugly complications later on. After all, they could prove *him* a claim jumper, unless he got some unimaginable break. The three figures were motionless for a long time, but at last backed down, moving cautiously. It was almost dawn before they were out of sight and range.

As the day wore on, Helms leisurely moved his rifle pit from the center of the slide to a point under the north wall. Elkhorn Sneed had been missing, he thought, in the night prowl led by Bluegum Ides, and Helms thought he knew where Sneed had gone. Consequently he was able to watch sardonically when, in the middle of the morning, a scatter of bullets cracked down from the rimrock a thousand feet above into his position of the day before. For half an hour the unseen rifle talked angrily, raking rocks and corners where Helms might have been, but was not.

Bluegum tried another advance at noon. Four men came up this time, not crawling now, but walking upright, cat-footed, shoeless, with bleeding feet. Bluegum, figuring that Helms had now been without sleep for forty-eight hours unless he slept by day, was trying the latter assumption. Helms waited until Ides was within four hundred yards, then sent a shot winging over their heads.

"Go on home!" he shouted contemptuously. Then he lay flat on his back in his rifle pit, rolling a cigarette while a dozen shots slammed into the rock around and over him. He poked his rifle over his barricade with one hand, and answered without looking. Once more he had outguessed Ides. When the counter-firing ceased, he looked down to find the four bolting down the slide in headlong retreat. For the first time in days, his face crinkled in a grin.

All day long he kept his watch, but although he sometimes saw figures moving far down the cañon, they did not come again. All night, too, the watch fire far below told him that the Ides outfit was there, but still they did not come on.

Then, at daybreak, a raking fire from rifles high above began combing Lon Helms's stronghold, and this time, besides a rifleman on the high north shelf that Elkhorn Sneed had used the day before, there was another high on the south wall — a position difficult to reach, but that Big Foot Scott had attained after many weary hours of toil. It commanded the base of the north wall. No longer was there a point on the rock slide from which a single man could hold off those advancing from below. The strong point of Crazy Woman's Cañon was untenable at last.

The rifles, however, swung their searching sights upon rocks only, naked and lifeless. During the night, foreseeing Ides once more, Helms had retired to his second line. Slowly, cautiously, Ides and O'Case skirmished their way up what little was left of the blind cañon above.

A quarter of a mile above, in a tight-winding gulch, lead spat at them from a nest of boulders, and Terry O'Case spun about and collapsed, shot through the thigh.

Now the slow fight took on an uglier, more savage note. Helms, with his back to the wall in the trap that his own stubbornness had built, was shooting at last. For two hours Ides himself exchanged shots with Helms at the longest range the twist of the cañon permitted. Ides got a broken hand from a shot glanced from the breech of his gun, but was still firing when Scott and Sneed came up to join him.

The beleaguers now began a slower and

surer advance, laboriously moving boulders ahead of them where natural cover was unavailable, forcing the fight to close range. At dusk they were close enough to begin looping broken rock into Helms's defenses. When this brought no reply, Ides shoved his hat into view, then risked his head. Once more Helms was gone.

With Ides it was no longer a question of merely taking possession of Lon Helms's discovery. The prospect hole rested unexplored by its takers. Furious as a wounded silvertip, he sought the man himself. Nor did he believe it possible for Helms to hold out much longer. Except for the long scaling switchback trail to the now blind Upper Shelf, there was little room for Helms to retreat again. Ides waited out the night.

By the light of morning the Ides rifles prowled what was left of Crazy Woman's Cañon, combing it cautiously. Lon Helms was gone.

Elkhorn Sneed made out a double speck that moved along the goat walk of the Upper Shelf. That was Lon Helms, leading his horse. Sneed and Bluegum Ides shook hands, grinning nastily.

Ides said: "He can't come down, and he can't get out. One of us will set here and gun him if he tries it back. He'll be a pretty starlight mark, working his way back down that bald granite!"

Leaving Sneed to watch, a mustached old he-cat at the trap mouth, Ides went cross-cañon, to have a look at the fortune he had captured.

"Call it the Fighting Jackass," suggested Big Foot Scott.

"Name it after *him?*" said Ides, nursing his smashed hand. "Hell, no! I'll call it the Gunsmoke . . . as an example to the next son-of-a-bitch stubborn upstart!"

High on the Upper Shelf, where that scarred edge of rimrock pinched off into the sliding at the edge of the Crush Cañon slide, Lon Helms mounted his horse and gauged the distance with his eye. Thus for a long time he studied the far reaches of Crush Cañon below. To abandon Crazy Woman's Cañon to the Ides outfit was a bitter wrench — although his water was gone, and his cartridges, and he was red-eyed and swaying in the saddle from loss of sleep, that fighting stubbornness of his was rampant still.

He could see now that it was time for him to go. Miles away, toward the mouth of Crush Cañon, he could make out a line of moving specks that could be nothing but a train of men and mules. A slow, ironic smile crossed his mouth, but left again as he regarded the Crush Cañon slide. This was a moment he had foreseen, and planned for, yet it found him shaky at the knees. Before him the slide of small broken rock gleamed white, a hundred-yard, down-striking band so steep that the mind could not understand its temporarily suspended motion. For a hundred yards below, the poised crag of rock hung on the dizzy lip of Crush Cañon, with nothing below but a thousand feet of empty space.

In his mind Helms had studied that slide, weighing the chances. He believed it true that no living thing could attack that balanced pour of stone without bringing it down in a mountain-shaking rush. But he had a theory. Once that slide started, a horse that tried to turn up it or across would be dashed and hurled into the abyss. But if a man boldly turned his horse *down* the slide, leaping diagonally downward with the sliding stones, he believed there was a chance that the horse could keep its footing, and reach solid ground on the other side before the roaring slip swept it over the drop.

It had seemed a sound plan, when he had conceived it, an audacious one, but within reason. With the slide before his eyes, it did not seem reasonable now, or possible at all. A cold sweat broke out on his face. He rolled a cigarette on the second try, and smoked it slowly. A dozen excuses occurred to him for turning away, postponing the plunge. But he knew that, if he did so, he would starve there before he ever faced the slide again.

Helms abruptly picked a spot three hundred yards below and across the slide, and forced his horse ahead. Slowly, fly-walking on stiff legs, the animal stepped onto the loose footing of the rock. Three slow quivering steps . . . five. Under the horse's feet the footing broke suddenly, and they dropped ten feet down the pitch as the slide gave away. The horse under Helms was half down, but fought for its footing, trying to turn back and up. The loosened rock from above smoked downward upon them, and the rock below ran from under the horse's hoofs. Helms wrenched the head of the horse downward, and slammed in the full gaff of the spurs.

In Helms's ears the roar of the slipping rock rose to a bellow, and a cloud of white rock dust exploded about him, so that he could not see where he went. Half the mountain had turned to a stone Niagara. He kept forcing the horse's head down, kept it leaping with the catapulting rock. The speed of their drop became impossible, bringing his stomach into his throat. For all

Helms knew he was galloping his mount straight over the tip of Crush Cañon itself. He shouted to his horse, but he could not hear himself in the roar of plunging stone. In that moment he believed he faced his death.

Then somewhere, on the edge of Crush Cañon itself, the horse found footing, and dragged clear of the clamoring stone. Well, it was over; that fool effort had been the keystone of his plan, and it was done. He rolled a cigarette.

Down below, in Crush Cañon, he met Jim Morton, coming in with his men and his mules behind him. Morton, red-faced and foxy, wrung his hand.

"Lon, I heard you were dead!"

"I doubt if they can prove it, Jim."

"I heard a bunch of truck. That you didn't record this claim . . . that it's been jumped and recorded on you, and you haven't any more mine than a rabbit . . . and that you were trying to jump your claim back, and were having a gunfight. . . ."

"Oh, that," said Helms.

"If you've brought me clear over here with my gang and my stuff for nothing. . . ."

"They jumped me, all right, Jim. But wait a minute. Did you happen to see a tall, saddle-colored Indian buck in overalls, with one ear clipped, as you came through Little Hat?"

"There was one like that drunk in the bar. But. . . ."

Helms drew a deep breath, and blew it out explosively. "That was a close one, Jim. That was Mono Logan. I gambled they would let him go get drunk, if I made it easy for 'em."

"But if they've recorded your claim on you. . . ."

"I guess I must have outguessed 'em, Jim. I stood 'em off in Crazy Woman's Cañon, just to keep 'em diverted, so they'd let Mono Logan off my back trail."

"And your strike?"

"Oh, that," said Helms again. "That's right over here in Crush Cañon."

THE BRAVER THING

To Dave Liggett's ears came what he took to be the whimper of a dog. He went to the door of his adobe-walled ranch house and whistled. The dusk had just turned into darkness only faintly moderated by the stars, and with the lamplight still in his eyes he could see but little beyond.

"Come in, Kentuck!" he sang out. "What ails you, dog?"

It was Saturday night, and a payday for the steady riders; Dave's three cowboys had gone to Redregon, so that the Wagon Wheel seemed uncommonly deserted and still. Out in the corral, a horse squealed, and Dave heard the *thump* of unshod hoofs on ribs, but there was no headlong doggy-rush at the open door. He whistled again, like a ground owl, and somewhere a real ground owl answered. Dave Liggett hesitated, experiencing the slightly foolish sensation of a man who has spoken to emptiness, then closed the door, and went back to his work.

Again, from somewhere outside, came

that faint, deceptive whine, and a third time, as Dave listened. He flung down his tally book, curiously uneasy. Once more he got up and flung open the door, whistling through his teeth.

Nothing answered him. The flat Southwestern plain lay singularly still under the vast bowl of the stars. For a minute or two he thought he heard the dog's panting, somewhere not far away, but the sound came no nearer, and presently he was sure he had heard nothing at all.

Now another sound caught his attention. A rider was coming in from the west at a high lope. He could hear plainly, after a moment or two, the rhythmic *thud* of a horse's hoofs upon the dusty soil. Dave waited, and, at last, after what seemed a long time, a bay horse, black-marked with runnels of sweat, pulled up just before him in the light from his open door. Instantly Dave's heart jumped, for the rider was Beth Warren.

"Kentuck get home?" she asked sharply before he could speak.

Ordinarily he would have caught her in his arms as she dropped from the saddle, for that was the way matters stood with them; she had promised to marry him, soon. But now the anxiety in her dark eyes startled him. Usually Beth Warren's eyes were warm and leisurely, smiling eyes that caught chance lights like dreamy waters; he had never seen them before in the shadow of a real alarm. "Why . . . why, no," he said. "What's happened?"

She seemed to have difficulty in finding words, and, when she answered, her voice was low and queer, as if the words hurt her. "He's . . . been shot," she said, looking him in the eyes.

For the space of perhaps one breath, Dave Leggett stared at her as if he did not comprehend.

"I saw it from a long way off," the girl was saying, rapidly now. "I was up on Three Crow Butte. I saw him fire, and Kentuck rolled, and then got up again . . . and he fired again, and Kentuck dropped . . . but after he rode off, Kentuck got up and started home. I rode hell-for-leather, Dave, honest, hoping to pick him up on my saddle, but dark closed down like a blanket thrown over me, and I lost him. I . . . I was hoping he got home."

"Just now . . . just a minute ago . . . I thought I heard him," said Dave, snatching a lantern from within.

The girl dropped from her horse, and together they searched westward from the house in half circles, calling Kentuck's name. And presently they found him, a small, shaggy, red-coated body, not a hundred paces from the door. As Dave leaned over him, Kentuck made a flopping noise with his tongue, such as a dog makes in going through the motions of licking a hand he cannot reach. Dave picked him up gently, but even as he lifted Kentuck, he felt the dog's body stiffen and quiver. All Kentuck's long, agonized struggle across the miles was wasted; he never reached the house alive.

When Dave had laid the dog upon his own bunk, Beth Warren, kneeling on the floor, threw her arms around Kentuck and buried her face in the shaggy red coat. She had loved this dog, not only for himself, but because Dave had loved him, and she loved Dave.

As for Dave — afterward he did not remember anger at all. It was something darker, more chilling, that possessed him as he sat down on a box and covered his face with his hands. He was already seeing that a new bit of history was as good as written into the story of the Redregon country. To make room for it, all his preconceived future, all his plans and hopes, had been abruptly struck away. He had realized suddenly that he was going to kill a man.

There was nothing explosive about Dave Liggett. Among the headstrong, self-sufficient cattlemen of the Redregon he was always the one to take the easy, compromising way. His good-natured grin and his flair for the humorous twist had kept the Wagon Wheel at peace with all his neighbors except one. It had not occurred to Beth Warren to mention the name of the man who had shot the dog Kentuck, nor had it occurred to Liggett to ask. Rufe Killion, owner of the Four Box to the west, was the only man in the Redregon who would have shot Dave Liggett's dog. If Beth Warren had not seen him fire, there would still have been no question.

Rufe Killion, although only forty, was a sort of hang-over from another day. He was no longer a true rustler, nor did his beginnings differ greatly from those of the other Redregon brands. In the tangle of the early days no man had built an outfit without gathering to himself a certain amount of loose stock. Only, Rufe Killion had been a late-comer; he got his start in a way that had already fallen into disrepute. He never carved notches in the grip of his gun, but the invisible notches were there, and many a rider remembered cattle branded with Killion's Four Box in a mighty peculiar way.

All that was nearly over with now. Killion no longer had any need for the old ways. He had a strong outfit, and he kept it strong. But the rough-shod, long-horned character behind it had not changed. Rufe Killion was never so much himself as when domineering it over lesser outfits and lesser men. "Keep your damn' hands off Devil Springs. That's Four Box water." "Keep your damn' riders off Gallos Bench . . . I'm sick of this prowling on Four Box land." "If you don't like it, start something . . . start anything any time, or right now!" That last was more than an invitation; it was almost a plea.

Rufe Killion had two brothers, Jake and Lee, no more than colorless shadows of the older man, but very nasty in any quarrel that Rufe backed. And his cowboys — there were from three to ten of them, according to the season — were mostly saturnine, misfit men, unable to get along with any boss they did not fear. A sweet pack, always ready to bully, to start trouble, to make work for better men. It was always a Four Box rider at the bottom of a shooting scrape, or a doubtful matter of brawling. And no one had suffered more repeated, petty annoyances than the Wagon Wheel, where Dave Liggett pursued his easy policy of give and take.

Liggett knew what Killion was after, all right. Twice before Killion had added vast grasslands to the Four Box range by hard crowding of new brands. By constant encroachment Killion had whittled down Tom Tryon's Lone Star brand until little was left but debts, when Tryon at last drew on Lee Killion and died with his gun in his hand. And he had broken the heart of Old Man Milam, who at last upped stakes and dragged. Over the lands of both the increasing herds of the Four Box had flowed, a rising tide. The Wagon Wheel now barred the next logical expansion of the Killion brand.

Already Dave Liggett had sustained a thousand minor grievances: here the skeleton of a cut pony, coyote-polished in a draw; there a shortage in the back-range calves; cut fences, missing cattle, Wagon Wheel water holes sucked dry by driven Four Box herds. His labor turnover was something awful. Yet he had managed, somehow, to hold his own.

All these things were in Beth Warren's mind, as Dave Liggett got up and walked, with the curious stiffness of a partly drunken man, to the peg where his gun belt hung. She watched him with wide eyes as he strapped the weapon on, but although her lips parted wide, as if she would have cried out, no word came.

She had never before seen in Dave Liggett's blue eyes the infinitely hard somberness that was in them now. Whatever it was within Dave Liggett that had always held him to his even, steady way had suddenly snapped and was gone, and she saw that, unless there was immediate intervention, either Rufe Killion or Dave Liggett would be dead before morning.

Suddenly she was on her feet and gripping Dave's shoulders. In her eyes was an intensity that held him motionless for a moment, even in his black mood. "Dave! You mustn't do it!"

He stood looking out over her head through the open doorway, westward into the dark. "I've had enough," he said, his voice very low, but thick and strained.

"Dave, you listen to me!" she commanded him. She tried to shake his shoulders, but it was like shaking a snubbing post or a log wall. Panic came into her voice, and her words tumbled over each other. "You don't know what you're doing. You're no gunfighter, Dave. He'll down you before your gun ever leaves the leather! Didn't he kill Pete MacPherson and Marty Hepner and old Paddy Andreen? All good six-gun men,

Dave. And you . . . you. . . ."

"I know," he said in that queer, constricted voice.

"Even if you downed him, his brothers would have you in twelve hours. And the law, Dave . . . he owns the Redregon law! Everyone knows Sheriff Murray is just his hired man. They'll. . . ."

"I'm not worrying about Dogie Murray," he said. He took her hands from his shoulders — neither gently nor roughly, but as if she had been a chair in his way.

She cried out: "Dave, where are you going?"

"Redregon. He'll be in Redregon, like everybody else on payday of a Saturday night."

A white terror was in Beth Warren's face. She had never seen a shoot-out, but she knew what they were. She could picture the moil of men in big hats and high-heeled boots in some Redregon saloon; the stampeding trample and rush to get out of line as the guns whipped out; the smash of exploding powder; and the quick reek of gunsmoke mingling with the whisky fumes as the crowd knotted above a fallen form that this time was going to be Dave.

Beth slammed the door and set her back to it. "Are you crazy? He'll be drunk, Dave!

Are you going to shoot a drunken . . . ?" She thought that her last argument had taken effect, for he hesitated. "At least, wait until morning," she begged. "Wait until. . . ."

"You're right," he admitted. "Tomorrow will be better."

What appalled her was that he was in no flurry of anger that could be expected to pass off in the night, but deliberate and cold. She saw that just as nobody had been able to stampede him before, nobody was going to be able to turn him now.

"It's in the cards, Beth. I guess I always knew this would come."

She made a final effort. "Dave, if you love me . . . you do love me, don't you, Dave?"

"God knows I do, Beth."

"Then, Dave, for my sake, won't you give this up?"

"It's in the cards," he said again.

"Then, at least, promise me you won't do anything until I talk to you again."

He shrugged. "He'll be driving home late in the morning," he figured. "I'll be riding west about noon."

"I'll ride by here at noon. You won't leave until noon?"

"Noon's all right, I guess," he said, his eyes on the floor.

She stared at him, finding it hard to comprehend that this was not the man she had known. A sob caught in her throat as she fumbled with the latch of the door, then she whisked out into the dark, and was gone.

Afterward Dave Liggett found out exactly how the news had run all over the Redregon country in the course of the night, but at first, as he waited for the long morning to pass, he had no inkling that anybody except Beth Warren knew that he had determined to kill his man.

Scotty Collins was the first to arrive, a small, peppery man with a grizzled mustache. Scotty's Two Z lay-out was the next outfit in the north. He came and sat beside Dave.

" 'Tis the Sabbath," said Scotty at last. "You ought not to set out to kill a man on the Sabbath, Dave."

"Who told you I was going after Rufe Killion?" said Dave.

"The word has got out," said Scotty. "Buck's coming in when he gets his chores done. Lem went to town last night, but I've sent for him. The Two Z is going to back your play."

"I don't ask anybody to back me," Dave said. "Draw back your chips, Scotty. This is my own hand."

Scotty Collins sighed. "Well," he mumbled, "I'll set and rest a bit, anyway." Silence fell, broken presently by hoof beats as three horsemen rode up — Lars Iverson and two cowboys, red-eyed and edgy from their night in town.

Iverson, tall, gaunt and bony-faced, joined Scotty Collins and Dave Liggett on the gallery of the adobe, while his two cowboys took the horses to the corral.

"Something on your mind, Lars?" asked Dave.

"I'm backing Scotty's play."

"You fellows," snapped Dave, "can just as well go roll your hoops. When I leave from here, I'm going alone."

Once more Scotty Collins sighed. "Well . . . we'll see."

A little column of dust was rising to the southwest on the Redregon road, and, even as Scotty spoke, they began to hear the rattle of an unregenerate engine. When a long, powerful old ark with a fluttering top at last pulled up beside the ranch house, it was Pat Cahill, owner and boss of the Lazy K, who swung down from the wheel. A gentle, snoring sound was audible from the back seat, from which three pairs of worn, high-heeled boots protruded at various somnolent angles. Two other cowboys climbed

224

down from the front seat and moved off to join Lars Iverson's men at the corral.

Pat Cahill was a genially blustering man with freckled, hairy hands, and bushy eyebrows above intense blue eyes.

"Dave," he said, "I'm glad it's come. These Killions was bound to hit into it sooner or later. Better to have it done with once and for all."

Dave Liggett's hackles began to rise. He was moved to announce hotly that he did not need assistance, but he was confused by the fact that these men were his friends, wishing him well, standing with him against his enemies. He fell silent, uneasy and uncertain.

That was a strange day. Hourly Dave's exasperated confusion grew as more men kept appearing, quiet men, wearing weapons they well knew how to use. From all over the Redregon country they were coming, in twos and threes and fives. The thing was so exaggerated, so unexpected, that at one point Dave suspected that he was the victim of an untimely joke. He had to discard this theory, however, as, looking about him, he perceived that there was not a man here who did not hold some grievance against the Killions, from a beat-up in a bar fight to the suspected loss of stock.

But the surprise of the morning occurred when Len Ross, foreman of the Bar 20, arrived in a heavy touring car, bringing with him seven men. The Bar 20 operated clear over in Clark County, beyond the Redregon hills. Ross must have started long before daylight to have arrived at the Wagon Wheel before noon.

Ross strode forward to shake Dave Liggett's hand. "For Lord's sake, Len," said Dave, "what brings you all this way?"

Ross, looking around him, laughed shortly, without humor. "What brung us all?" he asked. "There's two or three of us from over in Clark with old scores against Killion. The least we can do, Dave, is to take the look-out seat."

"Len," said Liggett, his face hard, "you've wasted your trip."

"What do you mean by that, Dave?"

Pat Cahill stepped in. "Come on, Dave," he said, "show down your cards. There's twenty-five, thirty men here. Six brands are holding up their work. This business is costing money all over the Redregon, and Clark, too. Once and for all . . . is it true that you aim to jump Killion, or not?"

Dave shifted. "If you've heard I'm going to gun Rufe Killion, you've heard right," he said. He was looking like a man who has picked a pebble out of a mountain side and found he has started an avalanche. "I'll gun him if it's the last thing I do. But it's strictly a job of my own. I appreciate you fellows coming here, but I don't see that it's any of your affair . . . any of you."

"Oh, you don't?" said Pat Cahill. "Well, suppose you kill Rufe. You'll be needing three or four good men to stand the rest of his outfit off, won't you?"

"I'm going alone," said Dave. "That's final!"

"Just a minute," said Len Ross. "I think your play is plain damn' foolish, Liggett, but that's your business. But now the rest of us have got something else to talk over, seems to me."

"Looks that way," said Scotty.

"It comes to this," said Pat Cahill. "We can't horn in on Dave's play if he doesn't want us to. But I say we better be thinking about what we're going to do next, after Dave is down."

Dave Liggett saw that they had accepted his ultimatum: he was to make his play alone. Already they were cold-bloodedly going ahead on the assumption that he was as good as dead.

"We weren't ready for this," said Scotty

slowly. "Right now the Killions are at the height of their strength. But two years more would have seen them whipped. They had a hard time horsing the last election. I don't think they'll horse it again. Once the county courthouse is cleared out, the Killions are done."

"That won't help us now," said Pat impatiently. "If they rub out Dave Liggett, they'll rub his outfit out. Who runs this county? That's the question here. If we're beat here, we're beat at the next election, and some of us are beat for good. This county can't run half rustler and half straight."

"We've got no choice," said Lars Iverson thickly. "Either we got to clean out the Killions and the sheriff's outfit, and his deputies, and anybody else that wants to stand up to honest men, or we admit, once and for all, Rufe Killion's boss."

"It's fight," said Cahill. "We've stood enough. . . ."

Dave Liggett turned and walked away, his head in a black daze. The Redregon had long been ready for just such an outbreak, and many a good man would snuff out before the work of the next few days was done. "Bloody Redregon" had been the name of that country once, in a day long forgotten. "Bloody Redregon" it would be again, to-

228

morrow night, in a thousand newspaper headlines. Yet he saw that the logic of the cowmen was inevitable, as inevitable as his own shoot-out with Rufe Killion.

Now Pat Cahill came to him where he stood apart. "You aren't the only one's got rights," he said. "We want to know what you're going to do."

"I've got Jimmy Hopper and Ed Leach posted on Three Crow Butte," said Dave. "From there they can see the road to the Four Box. Soon as Killion gets back from Redregon, they'll bring me word, and I'll ride."

"And if he doesn't get back before night?"

"I'll hunt him out in Redregon."

Pat Cahill turned away to take his message back to the leaders. The owners and the horses had appropriated the house. Dave's ranch, his affairs — even his life, when he came to think of it — had passed out of his control.

Now a rider was coming in at a high lope, and this, when he dropped from his horse, turned out to be snub-nosed Jimmy Hopper who, with Ed Leach, had been watching the Redregon road.

"Killion back?" Dave demanded.

"Not Rufe, he isn't," the boy reported.

"Then why are you back here?"

"There's been eleven cars gone up to the Four Box! Dogie Murray's gone up, and his three deputies, and Bill Akerman with four of the boys from the Crazy B, and Tom Fogarty with five more of the Arrowhead fellers, and. . . ."

"But you're sure Rufe Killion didn't go up?"

"Dead certain."

"Take some grub back to Ed Leach. Keep on watching," Dave told him.

"What the devil's the meaning of that?" Pat Cahill demanded when the boy had gone. "Do you suppose they've heard . . . ?"

"If twenty-five or thirty men know a thing, the world has it," said Len Ross contemptuously. "They know we're here. They've called to their wolves, same as us."

"Good," said Pat Cahill. "So they want fight, do they? We'll go into them like hell-fire through a haystack!"

"But where's Rufe Killion?"

They got no further light on that point until late in the afternoon, when Ham Davison, Bar W foreman, drove up at last, bringing fresh word. Old man Warren was still in Vegas, but Beth Warren was with Davison, and in the back seat were three more Bar W cowboys to add to the forces of war. Beth's face was pale and nearly expressionless as she looked over the throng, but Dave Liggett she did not appear to see.

Ham Davison stepped down from the wheel of the car. "Boys, all hell's on the drive, a-wheel and a-horseback! We're in for it for sure!"

"What's loose?"

"Rufe Killion has picked up the word. Every border-liner in the country that has ever cut in with him on a shady deal is rallying around to him now. The sheriff has gone out with his whole gang, and the Circle Buck, and the Flying U from clear over in Washita, and God knows who all . . . all swarmed up at the Four Box, with their guns flopping around their knees!"

"Well, we knew that much," said Pat Cahill dryly.

"They've read our play, and they've called our hand. The minute Dave touches off the powder, we're up against the damnedest fight the Southwest has ever seen. And if the Four Box water hole doesn't run red before morning. . . ."

"How does Rufe Killion take it?" asked Scotty.

Ham Davison leaned forward. "I tell you," he said impressively, "I tell you . . . *that man is scared.*"

"Go tear up your hat," said Cahill. "That

sidewinder scared? With that bunch of tough buckaroos around him?"

"They don't figure. What happens first of all? Dave will come walking in there, quiet and slow, through the crowd, and, before ever any other gun is drawn, Dave will be calling Rufe Killion out, and Rufe will have to go. That's the minute he hates to think about."

"Most like he'll have Lee plug Dave in the back."

"How can he do that, with his whole gang watching him?"

There was a short silence. "By heaven!" exclaimed somebody. "Do you suppose Dave can walk in there and get that buzzard before the rest slam him?"

"Liggett down or up," roared Pat Cahill, "we'll ride over that bunch like a prairie fire in August."

Dave Liggett heard all that, from where he sat apart from the rest. He had taken to whittling, and all afternoon his eyes had been down as he whittled the hours away. There was a big pile of shavings at his feet, and the hours, too, were behind, for across the plains from Three Crow Butte he now saw the hard-running horses of Ed Leach and Jimmy Hopper. Rufe Killion, he knew, was home.

He stood up and stretched, and his gun hung heavily against his thigh, as heavy as the unexpected weight of what he was about to do. All day his pony had stood beneath the cottonwoods, loose-cinched. He walked to it and jerked tight the latigo.

Everyone was watching him now. He turned his eyes to Beth Warren and found that she was looking at him for the first time since her return to the Wagon Wheel. She had stepped out of the car and stood poised, as if she had started to run to him but had found that she could not, and he noticed how dark her eyes were in her white face.

He had never seen her eyes darker than they were now, and there was an emotion in them that denied the expressionless calm of her features. Suddenly he realized that Beth Warren's eyes were darkened by a fear, a haunting horror.

"Bloody Redregon," he whispered. His eyes rested for a moment on Lars Iverson, and a picture came into his mind of Iverson's three tow-headed kids, watching wide-eyed as Lars was carried in by silent men, a blanket over his face. Lars had no business here. Then suddenly he realized that there were not three men in all that company who had an honest right to lay down their lives in lawless fight. They were blind, stubborn men, loyal and game, and they believed themselves confronted by an unevadable challenge. By a curious freak of fate, all these men were waiting for Dave Liggett — almost the youngest of them all — to make the move that would plunge the Redregon into feud.

But if, instead, he only withheld his hand. . . .

Stark terror swept him. Rufe Killion he did not fear, nor the smoke of guns. But now he asked himself if he dared be called yellow by these men, before all the Redregon, before Beth Warren herself. A cold sweat appeared on his forehead.

Ed Leach and Jimmy Hopper came hammering in on their lathered ponies.

"He's there!" Jimmy shouted. "Rufe Killion's home!"

There was a brief silence. Then two or three came forward slowly to Dave Liggett. "Well, good bye, Dave," Scotty Collins said, extending his hand. "Don't hurry your draw."

Dave Liggett did not shake hands. He put a hand on Scotty's shoulder and gently pushed him aside.

"Listen, you," his voice rose, and it was strong and hard, in spite of his conviction that he was never going to be able to hold his head up again. "You listen, all of you! Last night I made up my mind to kill a man. It was no business of yours. But you had to horse your way into my game. You weren't asked in, you horned in, dead set on turning a one-man shoot-out into a range war. All right, you can do what you want, but you got no starting gun from me! When I figure the time is ripe to go get Rufe Killion, I'll get him all right, and I'll ask no help from you. Now you go on home. I'm playing a lone hand, and there's going to be no shoot-out tonight. Get that, and like it, and to hell with you all!"

Silence fell, deep and heavy. He knew that it had never occurred to those men that Dave Liggett would back down. He supposed that, as they stared at him, they were trying to comprehend his inconceivable cowardice. He was the only one there, perhaps, who would ever know what it had cost him just to back down. He faced them silently for a long minute while they stared.

"We clear out," suggested Pat softly, "and you go ahead over there when we're gone? And have it look like the rest of us turned tail and went over the ridge?"

"Stick around, then, if you don't believe me," said Dave. "There's a case of whisky under my bunk. Somebody haul it out, and we'll see how it goes."

He turned his back on them and walked off into the twilight. Behind him an angry gabble arose from furiously disappointed men who had come to see battle. It was true that most of them thought Dave had turned yellow, and at the last moment had found his feet too cold to go on.

Presently in the shadows, three people met and shook hands three times around. They were Beth Warren, Ham Davison, and Scotty Collins. "I knew he would," said Beth, the tears running down her cheeks. "I knew he would, once he saw what it meant."

"I thought he would myself," said Scotty. "Girl, we've saved twenty murders today, by working it just this way."

"It sure took a lot of trouble, but we swung it," Ham Davison exulted. "Do you suppose any of these old hell-roarers realize we got them here just so Dave *would* back down?"

"No," said Scotty, "they don't. But, you know, for a little while there I thought we'd stirred up more hell than Dave would have the sand to stop. It took sand for that boy to back down then."

"He's got sand aplenty," Beth Warren declared. "He's got everything, that boy has."

As the whisky began to work, there were others — a good many of them — who began to feel that, after all, flowing liquor was better than flowing blood. Only a few belligerents remained irreconcilable when, long after dark, the cars began to pull away.

Except for Scotty, who was going back by saddle, the Bar W car was the last to go. Scotty shook hands with Beth Warren once more. "It sure took a pile of folks, and a pile of trouble, and a pile of wasted time to head off that killing," he said. "There's been a lot of money lost in the Redregon today, figuring the work that's been let alone and all, but it was worth it, I guess."

"You bet it was worth it," said Beth fervently. The light of melting stars was in her eyes.

When the last of them had gone, Dave Liggett went into his house and lighted a lantern. Wearily he started out his door toward the corral. And then. . . .

A shot smashed out of the darkness, and a spurt of flame showed at the corner of the corral. Rufe Killion, they later learned, unable to wait for Dave to come and get him, had come for Dave. He had come through the shadows, leaving his horse a long way out, and in the shadows he had waited his chance to plug Dave by the light of Dave's open door. The lantern crashed and went out as Dave Liggett went down with a smashed leg.

Twice more the ambushing gun spoke from the corral, while the ponies within trampled and milled. The third shot drew a touch of blood from the skin of Dave Liggett's neck.

Then, from where Dave Liggett lay, his own gun spoke once, and, after a painful pause, once more. At the corner of the corral there was a dead rattle of falling steel against logs, and Rufe Killion slumped to the dust and lay still.

Scotty Collins came tearing back, his pony stretching it at a dead run. At the sound of the first shot he had known instantly that all their hard riding, all their planning through the long night before, had been wasted in the face of a thing that was bound to be. He flung himself to the ground, without checking his horse, beside Dave's sprawled form.

"Dave! Did you get him, Dave?"

"Why, sure, Scotty," said Dave's strained voice. "Wasn't it in the cards all along?"

SUNDOWN CORRAL

Hidecamp cowboys liked to tell about what they called the fight at the Sundown Corral, but they get most of it wrong, because the Sundown Corral was no corral at all, just a hitch rack back of Kelly's, and the fight wasn't there, anyway, but rather all over the town. And they can't tell you why the fight changed Torch Breen as it did, because they didn't know.

Torch Breen was a big, hulking figure with a bush of wiry red-gold hair, hardly ever cut; long horse-bowed legs from nearly twenty years, man and boy, spent in the saddle; and the swift, sure judgment of a well-advanced boy of seven. When he was half drunk, the red blaze of his hair was matched in his eyes. There was a sort of angry glory about the arrogance of Torch Breen in liquor.

But after his fight with the Kettlesons he hung up his gun, drank seldom and sparingly, and brawled with no one. Later he even married. He married a girl from the East who worked in the kitchen of Kelly's restaurant, had a kid of her own, and called herself Mrs. Smith. The cowboys, in their innocence of mind, supposed the kid to be Torch's, since both Torch and the kid had red hair. This was untrue. But, anyway, Torch built a cabin on a section of land, and became a thing of the past completely.

His aggrieved friends felt that the Kettleson fight hardly explained it. It was true that throughout the fight Torch Breen had chiefly shown an inflexible determination to get away. Yet even in retreat he had done so much damage, against odds so great, as to make a name for being poison to fool with. No sense in his coming out of it spirit-broke, like that.

Without knowing just how it started, everybody knew that Torch Breen and the Kettlesons were openly on the gun. Still, both sides avoided meeting — until that smoky twilight when Torch Breen, along with Shanty Simms, walked square into the Kettlesons, all six of them, clamped along the rail of the Point-of-Rocks Bar.

Breen's gun jumped into his hand, and there was a mighty long minute of quiet while Torch waited for them to make their play. They made no play.

Torch said: "Come on, Shanty." He kept his gun on the Kettlesons while the two backed out of there. Once outside, Torch and Shanty made a dive for Hawk's store, next door. Just as they made it, Guy Kettleson sprang to the door of the Point-of-Rocks; his gun spoke, and Breen's answered.

Torch Breen's shot smashed Guy's arm, but Torch and Shanty didn't know that. Shanty shouted: "Every man for himself . . . there's a million of 'em!" And both ran out of the back of Hawk's store, meaning to cut north behind the buildings to the Sundown Corral — that unfenced hitch rack back of Kelly's restaurant — where their ponies were. It was the worst thing they could have done. Buck and Willie Kettleson were waiting for them back there, barricaded behind a pile of whisky kegs. There was a swift fusillade. Buck got a busted leg from a slug that somehow filtered through the barrels, and Willie got his face cut by a jumping splinter. Willie always was easily satisfied.

"Gee," Shanty whimpered, "we're surrounded." He and Torch dived into the back end of the Muleskinner Saloon and ran through to the front.

Wham! Dee Kettleson had swung himself up onto the roofs, where he could command front and rear, and, as Torch and Shanty appeared in the street, he fired over Hawk's false-front parapet.

Both Torch and Shanty returned his fire. As their shots crashed through the flimsy clapboards, Dee Kettleson jerked straight upright, pitched forward over the parapet, and rolled down the wooden awning to fall heavily into the street.

"We're done for," Shanty Simms moaned. "They're everywheres." Four Kettlesons were out of action now, but Dee Kettleson was the only one Torch had seen fall. Where the other five were he had no clear idea. They ducked back through the line of buildings and turned north again, yearning for the Sundown Corral and their waiting horses.

Boom! Another miracle as Lloyd Kettleson missed. Lloyd, guessing where their ponies were, had placed himself while Torch and Shanty were settling with Dee in the street, and now blazed away from cover of a wagon shed. One of Torch's answering bullets ricocheted off Lloyd's gun, breaking three bones in Lloyd's hand. Five Kettlesons out of action! But. . . .

"We're headed off!" Shanty gasped. "Torch, we got to fight through this solid wall of Kettlesons! It's our only hope!"

So they charged straight on this time, from time to time tossing a shot in this direction or that, picking off imaginary Kettlesons. They reached the Sundown Corral, all right.

But Torch Breen went berserk now. He wheeled, facing back the way they had come, and he wasn't in a hurry any more. His eyes had a crazy red blaze as they swept the ramshackle backs of the wood buildings. Nothing moved there at first, anywhere. Then, in a pile of boxes behind Kelly's restaurant, Torch saw one big packing case move, as if someone stealthily had crept forward to its cover from the corner of the unpainted wall.

Torch Breen blasted a bullet through the box at twenty yards, and would have fired again, but the hammer snapped upon an empty shell. Torch snarled crazily and charged, immune to sense, immune to fear. He snatched the big packing case aside, and his gun barrel flashed up for a skull-cracking, hand-to-hand smash. It would have been suicide, and the end of him, if a Kettleson had been there.

Nobody was behind the box. Torch hesitated, swearing futilely. He started to turn away. Then Shanty Simms saw him freeze. Breen stood motionless, caught in mid-step, almost.

Shanty kept gibbering for Torch to come

on, and, when Torch still stood there, seemingly unable to hear, Shanty spurred his
pony over to Torch, meaning to drag him
bodily away. But Shanty also froze when he
looked down into the box, forgetting their
situation.

In the bottom corner of the box — overturned there when the box overturned —
huddled a little girl perhaps three years old.
Both thumbs were in her mouth, and she
rolled her eyes up at Torch Breen without
moving anything else — too scared to move,
too scared to cry. Her hair was red, like
Breen's, only brighter, and a finger's
breadth above the shine of that hair they
could see the .45 caliber hole Breen's shot
had made in the thin wood.

After a couple of moments a woman ran
out of the back door of the restaurant. It was
the woman who called herself Mrs. Smith.
She was young, but she was pitifully thin,
and she always had a hunted look, and now
she looked scared to death, too, so that she
looked fifteen years beyond her age. She
caught up the child, and for just half a
second stared at Breen with eyes full of re-
pugnance and terror, then ran back inside.

Torch Breen still stood there, his face the
color of something from under a board, so
that he looked like a dead man stood up.

Even his gun looked dead, dangling in his hand with the look of a lead gun, not meant to be fired, and the hand that held it looked dead, as if unable to lift it, even to put it away. Only his hair looked alive, shining like something burning, in the failing light.

THE BELLS

OF SAN JUAN

Whiskers Beck's fan-like spread of white beard was damp and draggled. Above it his mustache stuck out in disgruntled wisps, like the fur of a drying cat. He ran a blue bandanna over his bald head, and his tired hand fell away lackadaisically, leaving the handkerchief perched there in a soggy wad.

From their bench by the bunkhouse door the Triangle R cowpunchers gazed across the broad Wyoming prairie, steaming from its fresh rain. The vapor floated thinly, close to the ground, obscuring the feet of the far mountains. It had been a welcome rain, like a last farewell of the spring that had but a little while ago lost itself to dry heat. It would put fresh power into the grass, add many a hundred weight of flesh to the Triangle R herds, but to Whiskers Beck the downpour had been a vicissitude. He had ridden all day, chilled, coatless, dripping in rivulets. By the time he reached the main ranch again, a new leak in the roof had seen to it that he had no dry clothes to put on. Now he sat, drying slowly and thinking of better things. From out in the horse shelter the wheeze of an accordion came through the dusk, accompanying a thin song.

The bells of Saint Mary's
er callin', er callin',
The bells of Saint Mary's, tiddly um
tum to me. . . .

The accordion's wail suited Whiskers's mood. His mind was turning to younger things, to a place mildly warm where the song of bells really rang over a far, dry land. In the smoke of his cigarette he could see a white plain, still sending up heat waves in elusive rainbow shimmerings, even in the twilight.

A placid expanse of water is held by a dam at the bend of the Pipestone River. Sedges, grass, and willows grow lush at its edge, long after the rest of the land is sere. By the bright water sit the flat-roofed little houses of San Juan, their blue and pink and yellow adobe reflected so clearly that it seems other houses are hanging head downward in limpid depths. The little plaza they enclose is shaded by four or five big trees; their twisted arms rise protectively over the tiny town. There is a well in the plaza, its deep waters crystalline and cool. And in the haze of evening the smell of cooking drifts through the village, the steaming aroma of fríjoles con carne *and chili's tantalizing pungency. . . .*

"I don't know what I'm goin' to do with Tar'ble Joe," said Dixie Kane, "if he don't leave off passin' out that cold salt jackfish. Here we come in all holler an' soaked, an' what loud smell brings us up standin'? Damn' dead fish again an' not even warm. I never seen such a thing in a cow country. I know the Old Man bought that jackfish cheap, an' it's like to spoil, but. . . ."

Whiskers winced and let the sentences drift meaninglessly past his ears.

At one side of the plaza stands the ancient mission of San Juan. Its adobe is falling away, revealing the deep maroon of its mortar, the venerable gray of its stone. Its arches are weathered, seasoned, more beautiful with the years. What lost fragment of a Penitente religion is surviving here? Who are the dark-faced, black-robed monks? What are the words of their chanted prayers? A man doesn't recall.

At evening the bells of the mission peal in mellow tones. There are only six of them in the squat bell tower, but the man who plays them makes them seem like many more. Some of the chimes are not in key. There is a wild plaintiveness in the songs they sing, a tale of something not quite complete — as if they bear kinship to Indian water drums, Navajo robes at once vivid and subdued, and such almost forgotten things. Sweet bells, though, sweet in the evening twilight. . . .

"Gosh," said Dixie, "y'oughter see the swell mud in the corral. Tomorrer, if yun see bubbles comin' up to the top, sink a rope down . . . it's me lookin' fer m'horse. I hope it rains all week."

"Amen," said Whack-Ear heartily. "Drizzle, drazzle, squnch, squnch, squnch . . . ain't that music?"

Whiskers, with great effort, dragged himself out of Whack-Ear's imaginary mud. He turned his ears to the accordion, and his mind to far off San Juan.

In the evening under the trees in the plaza dark-eyed girls stroll arm in arm, and youths in bright serapes, their conical, wide-brimmed hats cocked jauntily, lounge here and there with their cigarettes and watch the girls. A man doesn't remember it all. What were the winged things that lived in the tower with the bells — bats, or owls — or something else? And what were the odd, big-billed birds that nested in the plaza, sending strident bugle tones through the midday heat?

There is life, and love, and color in San Juan, to say nothing of the cooking of Madrecito Pasqual. But these things are only decorations for a place of warm peace, where an old man can sit and smoke and rest his rope-gnarled hands. Mornings, no crawling out of bed into the cold dark, no labor stretching ahead to the day's end. Evenings, a chair against a hut by the plaza, a smell of hot food, and the song of the vesper bells. They only work when they feel like it, in San Juan. . . .

A banjo with a tin head, a set of tinware drums, and four galvanized voices suddenly burst into self-expression at Whiskers's elbow.

**Ching lang ling, ching lang ling,
Ching la dee dee!
Sweet were the words that she hollered
at me!
Ching lang ling. . . .**

"Holy murder!" Whiskers moaned. Slowly he went inside, where he pulled damp blankets over his aching head. *What I need is a vacation,* he told himself. *And by*

God I'm goin' to take it!

South, southwest by the clicking rails, south to the *casitas* of San Juan. . . .

For an hour and a half the little tin car had jounced its way along twisting ruts in a glare of sun, but, as Whiskers stepped stiffly to the ground, the sun suddenly completed its drop behind the ranges, and earth and grass merged into a barren of veldt as gray as his dust-matted beard. He should have arrived at San Juan earlier, but because of an inaccuracy in his railroad map Whiskers had got off fifteen miles too soon. Since no more trains were due, he had had to travel twenty-four miles by flivver instead of the eight miles expected. For a while he stood there in the dust beside his telescope valise.

At the end of a full minute he said: "Can this be . . . ? Oh, I guesso." After two minutes he said: "Seems like I must 'a' kind of fergot this here smell of sheep. Mebbe it won't seem so plumb outstandin', come mornin'." There was a slightly pained expression about his eyes but a fine flourish in his voice as he told himself: *Well, gosh . . . it's great to be back!*

A stir of excitement was animating the figures that lounged against the huts facing the square. They drew together into groups;

they jabbered in hushed voices, covertly gesticulating. A ragged youth with a puffy brown face was approaching timorously. Through the Mexican's straggling forelock, Whiskers discerned the glint of terror.

I got a big notion to make a face at him, said Whiskers to himself, *jest to see him leave his clo'es behind in one clean jump.*

"Ah, *buenos tardes, señor capitán,*" the youth quavered huskily. He continued in Spanish: "All is in readiness."

"What?" snapped Whiskers. The dark youth quailed, then turned and ran bowleggedly. "Stop!" Whiskers yelled. The young man stopped. "Come back here!" He came creeping back. The groups before the colorless adobe shacks had grown swiftly; probably everyone in the village was watching. "Take this valise!" He now took to his half-forgotten Spanish. "Take it to the house of Madrecito Pasqual. No! Pasqual. *Pasqual.* P-a-s-k-o-l . . . Pasqual."

The valise flopped into the dust again, and bony hands spread deprecatingly. A torrent of frightened Spanish slithered forth. What *el capitán* asked was impossible, Whiskers was told. La Madre Pasqual was dead. Her old man was dead. Her sons were either hanged or run away. Her house was now the jail. He would be only too glad to see *el capitán* comfortable in it, but it was occupied already. But if only *el capitán*. . . .

Whiskers Beck silenced the outpouring with difficulty. "Oh, all right," he conceded, "take me somewheres else."

With something like a sob of relief the youth snatched up the canvas valise and trotted ahead, his bare feet flapping in the dust. Had he been less travel weary, Beck would have swaggered. Seldom had he attracted more awestruck attention. As he followed the *peon* past the huts on the side of the plaza, the inhabitants ahead of him withdrew into doorways, oozed around the corners of walls. He could feel eyes peering at him from windows and doorways ostentatiously vacant. Glancing over his shoulder, he could see the people timorously coming out of hiding to stare at his retreating back.

He whirled in his tracks, and the nearest reappearing group scuttled into hiding again. "Anyway," said Whiskers, "they know who's boss around here!"

They entered the largest of the adobe houses, and for a moment Beck could see nothing in the windowless dark. There was a close smell of sweat-drenched clothes baked by the dry heat, a chicken-coop odor from a corner where fighting cocks must have lived for years, and a smell of weak mutton stew that suggested boiled wool. Whiskers gasped for air.

" 'Sawful funny how a man fergets smells."

A baggy old woman was before him, bowing and making conciliating gestures. She mouthed bad Spanish with toothless gums.

"Give me a drink," he ordered.

A tin can was handed to him, and he raised it eagerly to his lips. Into his mouth flowed a lukewarm semi-liquid, too thick for water, too thin for mud. It tasted of pond slime and rusty tin. He spat the stuff upon the earthen floor, threw down the can, and booted it into the plaza. The *peon* who had carried Whiskers's valise leaped for the door and fled. The baggy old woman's apologies became tumultuous, profuse. It was evident that she had no other drink to offer, and Whiskers felt ashamed. Silently he went out in search of a saloon.

The clear, lasting light of evening lay coolly on San Juan, revealing none too kindly the hardships worked upon it by careless living. But Whiskers, made angry by his thirst, saw nothing but the thing he sought — San Juan's only bar. **Pulquería** its scaling sign advertised it, and Whiskers strode toward it across the plaza. As he pushed into the room's fetid heat, the reek of raw alcohol, supported by the peculiarly characteristic odors of Mexican liquors, for a moment gave him pause. He scowled redly about the room, fixing a stare of malevolence on each of its dozen patrons in turn. Then his silver rang on the bar.

"Best in the house!"

The white *aguardiente* whisky scorched its way down his throat, bringing tears to his eyes and starting a small bonfire in his empty middle.

"Gimme another."

He drank a second, and a third; then, as he turned to look about him, he discovered that the saloon was empty. At a little square window in the rear mud wall he could see four or five staring heads silhouetted against the evening sky. They immediately withdrew.

"Well, wha-at the hell here?" Whiskers wondered aloud. For the first time he began to notice something odd about his reception in San Juan. He pushed out into the better air of the plaza.

Sauntering, he began a general reconnaissance of this place to which he had chosen to come. As he checked over one after another of the things that had changed, a heavy mood of gloom descended over him with the lowering dusk. For San Juan, somehow, had shrunk. It was only a struggling handful of adobe shanties now, and the dusty sterility of the burnt desert had crept in. The gay pinks and blues and creams were gone from the walls of the huts, scoured and blasted to the color of dust by sirocco-lashed sand. The plaza, too, had shrunk in the heat of the years until it was only a sort of dusty yard, a place to throw tin cans, bottles, and old rags. Three of the four trees in the plaza were dead; only broken claws remained of their great, foliated arms. On the last living tree two or three limbs still bore a few handfuls of dusty leaves; the rest were sere. How small and twisted those trees seemed now that they were broken and forlorn! And the big-billed, piping bugle birds were gone. Beneath the broken trees the clear-water well was filled up, disused, a heap of garbage where it used to be.

Whiskers Beck pressed forward, feeling the urgent need of resting his eyes upon the coolly placid waters of the Pipestone. At first he couldn't find the Pipestone at all. There was, indeed, the dusty bed where it had been, but it seemed that even the Pipestone was now running upside down. Then, walking along the powdery bank, he came upon all that was left of that bright expanse of water. The dam was broken, washed away in freshets long ago. A few snaggle-teeth of drunken stakes, garnished with driftwood, were all that remained. Left unsupported, the broad pond had shrunk to a reeking puddle thick as gumbo. There was still green stuff growing about it — green, that is, in comparison to the parched plains cactus. It grew rank in the weltering mud. From this stagnant mud hole the *peones* scooped the dull water that they drank. It was wet enough, at least, to breed mosquitoes in swarms and clouds.

"Fer God's sake," said Whiskers Beck. "You could knock me over with a medium-sized axe!"

Scratching his mosquito bites, Whiskers made his way back into the plaza in search of the ancient mission. As he turned the corner of a hut, a ragged, pot-bellied child started up, stared at him, and fled screaming. Beck stopped to scratch his head.

They's a strap broke somewheres, he told himself. *They must think I've got some disgustin' disease.*

Once more, as he strolled before the huts, the lounging groups melted away at his approach to form again, staring, when he had passed. It was beginning to get on

Whiskers's nerves.

"Got a mind to make a feint at 'em," he grumbled, "an' have the town plumb to myself."

The little stone building that housed the mission had crumbled away. Its arches were broken, scourged by the sand. Its mysterious windows were notches in disordered stone. Its flagged floors, once worn smooth by the passing and re-passing of sandaled feet, were now open to the sky, heaped with windrows of dust. And the people — ragged, timorous, unwashed — where were the swaggering youths who once had galloped in from the plain, the silver decorations tinkling on the bridles of the shaggy, fighting ponies that they rode? Where were the dark-eyed girls who strolled in gay *mantillas* as the twilight fell beneath the trees? They had been beautiful then . . . vanished now, or turned to squat, ugly old women, picking over garbage in the square. And the bells — the bells were gone, as were the ringers, their tower crumbled away with the rest. Gone, gone, the mellow-voiced bells and all the beautiful remembered things, the threads of a vanished dream.

"I ain't goin' to make no statement," Whiskers mumbled, "not tonight. Nossir, not even to myself. But I *will* say, of all the cheap, low-down swindles I ever seen, that railroad ticket I bought to come here was the worst!"

He moped along, dragging his boots in the dust, toward the hut where he had left his valise. Whiskers Beck could not afterward distinctly recall just when or how he became aware that a rifle was looking at him from a window across the plaza. But when he did realize it, there was no room in his mind for doubt. Without seeming to look, he gave that window the careful scrutiny peculiar to men who think themselves likely to be shot. The dusk was thickening rapidly. A gunny sack partly obscured that black hole in the wall across the square. No one could have been certain that anything in particular was visible there. Yet the longer Whiskers studied the opening, the more certain he became that he could see part of a face, a bulge of shoulder, a dark-looking something on the window ledge that was hard to account for in peaceable ways.

Every peculiarity that he had noticed in the actions of San Juan's inhabitants returned to him in a tumbling parade. The red grouch that had been growing in him now swiftly cooled. Expecting momentarily to hear the hum of a bullet past his head, yet without quickening his pace, he reached the smelly hut to which he had first been led, hesitated for a fraction of a moment at the door, as if he were going to lean against the jamb to rest, then with one quick step put the wall of the hut between himself and the rifle — if it was a rifle — that watched him from across the open ground.

For a moment or two he stood against the hut's inner wall, accustoming his eyes to the new dark. When he had satisfied himself that he was alone, he cautiously peered out around the wooden jamb. At the window that he suspected he could make out even less than before; if anything, the gunny sack had been moved to shield it a little more effectively. No light had been lit in the building in question, or in those adjoining it, and the failing twilight gave his eyes little with which to work. When he had stood there motionless for some little time, a sharp thrill aroused him, and, although he made no move, his attention snapped from the window across the plaza to the darkness behind him, within the hut itself. Something had moved there, a rat, a scorpion — or a man. He had no gun, or any other weapon, unless the folding knife in his pocket could be considered such. Motionless, he waited for the sound to recur.

It came again, the smallest part of rustle,

the faintest hint of a tread. This time he thought he detected it in a suggestion of weight, telling him that whatever had moved possessed size and mass. He waited, scarcely breathing — waited. Suddenly Beck whirled and grabbed with both hands. His fingers closed on wrists. Then he let go and cursed, for the wrists were flabby and old. As he released them, that horrible baggy old woman sank to her knees on the mud floor and, reaching claw-like hands upward, pleaded volubly that he spare her life, if only long enough for her to get him his supper.

When at last he had got the shaking old woman to her feet, partially reassured that she was no longer in danger, Whiskers wiped the cold sweat off his forehead and demanded his valise. His remaining tobacco was in it. When he smoked again, he thought, perhaps he would be able to eat. He was furious with himself for his nervousness, for the foolish things that the bashfulness of these people had made him imagine. Stepping to the door, he exposed himself full front to whoever might be across the square with rifle or with none, and, when no shot came, he mocked himself the more.

"This way, *señor el capitán,* in this room here is your baggage, your bed, your supper,

261

everything. Ah, *señor,* we have done our best to make you comfortable and happy. Only walk this way, *señor.*"

"Bring a light, *señora.*"

"Ah, *sí, sí, señor,* only enter and make yourself comfortable. I will borrow a neighbor's light."

She shuffled out. Whiskers Beck blindly stepped through the door she had indicated into a stuffy room. He was feeling in all his pockets for his matches. A heavy body crushed down upon his head and shoulders with such impact that the tendons of his neck cracked, and he saw an illusory flash of light. He was borne down. His feet were swept from under him, and the floor rushed upward in an attempt to dash out his brains.

Deliberately, when the first daze of impact had passed off, Whiskers took stock of his situation. He was prone on the floor, clamped there by the weight of more than one heavy man. One eye was swelling shut from contact with the hard adobe on which he lay, but he believed that he was otherwise unhurt. He could hear congratulatory mutterings above him, and, as soon as he had made out that these were in English, he decided to await quietly the development of events. Beck was past the age where men struggle violently without definite purpose in view.

A strong hand jerked one of his wrists behind him, then the other. About each of them clicked a band of steel.

"Put on the leg chains w'ile yer at it," said a wheezy voice.

"What good is . . . ?" said a second voice.

"D'you think I wanter get kicked in the eye?"

"Oh, all right."

"What the highfalutin hell?" queried Whiskers Beck in smothered tones. "You think I'm so spooky as all that?"

"We know yer all right," said the breathy voice. "I'll jest set right here in the middle of his back, Ed, till you get them leg irons on. All set? Light the light then, an' shut the door."

A goodly glow of kerosene light flared up, revealing nothing to Whiskers except that the floor had not been swept lately.

"Gimme a hand, Ed," the wheezy man said. "Ain't so limber as I useter be. Heist up! *Oomph!* Reckon I fall jest as heavy as I ever did, though."

With the weight raised from the small of his back, Whiskers twisted his neck to peer upward at the man's huge bulk. "Hope t' see you fall heavier," he said.

"What's that?"

"I say," said Whiskers, "I never seen no one fall heavier."

"I reckon not," said the bulky one. "See if you can find his guns, Ed. Damn me if I can find even a bean blower on the cuss. Ain't that queer?"

Lean, strong hands rummaged through Beck's clothes. As they turned him over, Whiskers saw they belonged to a tall young man with a thin, sad face, a face whose defect was a peculiarly earnest expression.

Don't look real bright, Whiskers decided. The other man was of bulging oval figure, with a face, Whiskers thought, suggesting a Berkshire pig of political turn of mind. He was growing bald.

"Heist him up, Ed, onto that bench there. Let's have a look at him."

When the earnest young man had planted Whiskers as directed, the fat one arranged himself in a rickety armchair, placed his fingertips together, and contemplated the prisoner.

"Gosh, Mister Walker," said the man called Ed, "he don't look like such a tough one, does he?"

"He looks more like a man lookin' out of a hay pile," Walker offered. He studied Beck's dust-matted beard disparagingly. "But, then, you gotta consider that those whiskers ain't his own."

"An' you," said Whiskers Beck, "look somethin' like a cross between a cook wagon an' a balloon. Only I s'pose that four ton of fat ain't yours, neither."

"You won't get now'eres that way," said the fat man. He tapped a small nickel star that was pinned to his coatless suspenders. "His guns must be in his satchel, Ed. Crack her open."

They dragged open Beck's canvas telescope, and Ed began listing the contents in a singsong voice. "Bunch of old blue shirts, bunch of old overall pants, bunch of playing cards with a string tied 'round, bottle rheumatiz medicine, bottle of hair tonic, bunch of wool socks."

"Will that hair tonic work?" asked the fat one.

"Bunch of underwear, bunch of pitcher postcards, good light bridle, good pair boots, six-seven pair spurs, three apples, three an a half mouth organs, one boiled shirt . . . ain't clean, old rumpled black necktie, two tired-out high collars, muzzle fer a dog, sewin' outfit in a candy box, gold medal fer ridin', two rat traps . . . been used, bottle wolf poison, tin thing with a pitcher on it that goes over a stovepipe hole, medium-size fryin' pan, skinnin' knife, long piece red ribbon, brush an' comb, bunch of

all kinds of pipes, one skin off a cat, cigarette papers, mantelpiece clock, about forty
sacks Bull, colored pitcher of Niagara Falls,
gob of beeswax, bunch of keys, couple
dozen loose straps, bag of harness buckles . . .
I dunno what this here is . . . two Jew's-
harps, twisted-nail puzzle, shoe fer a mule,
axe head, piece buckskin, mail order cat-
alog, rattlesnake skin, string of silver
conchas, sea shell, cigar box of nails, sad-
dler's outfit, Injun pouch full of buttons,
china hen's egg. . . ."

"No guns ner dynamite ner nothin'?"

"Nope. Not unless it's dynamite wropped
in this newspaper. Ain't though . . . it's railroad spikes. Extry hatband, curb chain,
Spanish spade, double curb, hinge fer a
door."

"No use goin' no further," said the fat
man with the star, "the valise ain't his."

"Prob'ly stole it," Ed suggested.

"Most like. Not only that but stole it off
some pore, dodderin' old man that didn't
have good sense. Look at all that worthless
junk. Cat skins! Hens' eggs! Useless to anybody not foolish in the head. Ain't you
ashamed, now," he addressed Whiskers,
"takin' the playthings away from some pore
old has-been, prob'ly in his second or third
childhood? What do you think yer

repersentin' this time, anyway?"

Beck's old leather face had turned an angry maroon, but he swallowed his temper and answered mildly. It seemed to him that he smelled more *aguardiente* in the room than was accounted for by his own breath. "I'm a cabin boy on a ship," he growled.

The fat one suddenly dropped his ponderously playful attitude. His small gray eyes made a very fair attempt to gimlet Whiskers. "W'ere'd you leave your valise? An' your saddlebags? An' that sack?"

"Refuse to answer," said Beck, "on advice of counsel."

"This here's no laughin' matter," the other rumbled. "Them banditries of yours may be all very neat an' pleasant, but you've went jest a leetle too far. That man you killed happened to be the sheriff's brother. Now, look here. You come clean with me an' tell me where the stuff is, an' I'll see that you get a fair, square trial. Nobody never made a mistake by comin' clean with Cap Walker. If I'm with you, you got a chance. If I'm against you, you're in one hell of a fix, mister, an' don't you ferget it. Now you jest better. . . ."

"I don't know who you are, an' I don't give a damn!" said Whiskers. "That ain't all. You don't know who I am an' never seen me before in your life. Mark my words, you better be all-fired. . . ."

Walker waved an incredulous fat hand at Whiskers as he turned to Ed. "Would you believe it?" he demanded. "Jest because he's got some phony w'iskers on he thinks he's in disguise or somethin'. Jest like we couldn't know him plain by his eyes, an' nose, an' build, an' clo'es. Why, feller, we knew you was comin' here, an' from which way, an' when, before you ever started. Every Mex in the town was ready an' willin' to help us . . . they ain't forgot that Verdad affair, not by no means. Well, we'll jest have an end to his hidin' behind spinach, if that's what's holdin' the show back. Off they come!"

Tears of pain came to the old man's eyes — but the whiskers stayed. An amazed, unbelieving look spread over the fat man's whisky-flushed face. It was followed by a new determination. Walker seized Whiskers's beard with both hands and jerked once, twice, three times, each time harder than before. Then he bent over Whiskers and minutely examined the beard at its roots. Finally he stepped back and sat down.

"Ed," he said wheezily, with the air of one flabbergasted, "they're real. This ain't him at all. We're jobbed, Ed, jest plain jobbed."

Then, suddenly, he swelled like a cinched

burro. His brief eyebrows went up, his mouth opened, and he burst into soprano guffaws. Slowly, rustily at first, but with increasing celerity, the high, cackling laughter poured from him. He rocked in his chair, his face reddened; the tears appeared on his cheeks, and he held himself with flipper-like hands, as if fearful that he would burst. Now and again the laughter subsided to exhausted giggles, only to break forth again in renewed roars.

"The look," he gasped at last, "on his . . . face!"

Laughter again, and more laughter, till he shook like a great weak-hooped keg with a dog fight inside. The long lean young man viewed all with a uniform sadness. Whiskers, however, was boiling. The tip of his fan-like beard quivered, and on his forehead the veins stood rigid.

"Leave him . . . loose," gasped Walker at last.

Obediently the youth named Ed unlocked the handcuffs from the wrists of Whiskers Beck and put them in his pocket. Whiskers, his eyes quiet and gleaming now, studied the holstered Colt that sagged from the man's gun belt on the right, noted how the fat man with the star leaned limply against the wall, staying the last of his chuckles as best he

269

could and wiping his eyes with his handkerchief. The young man stooped to unlock the chain shackles from Whiskers's legs. The lock snapped free.

With his right hand Whiskers pressed the man's head down as he brought his own knee up with all his strength. The bony old knee caught the other between the eyes, and he slumped. Beck's left hand had already gripped the butt of the gun at the young man's belt. He changed the gun to his right hand as he sprang across the room.

"Feel *that?*" he demanded, prodding the gun into the fat man's stomach. And the other let his own gun drop back into its holster as his arms went above his head. Whiskers disarmed him. "Now put the handcuffs on your sorrowin' friend," he ordered harshly, "afore he wakes up. . . . That's good. Got another pair? Fine. Turn around an' stick your hands back. Now we'll jest harness your left leg to his left leg with these chain fixin's, so's you're shore goin' to do a close lockstep if you come out of here with 'em on. Now, gents . . . I'm right sorry you ain't got no whiskers to pull. An' I ain't got any paint, ner feathers an' m'lasses, to make you look any funnier'n you do now. So I guess I'll jest leave you here to think over how a pore, dodderin' old man that didn't have good sense come it over the two of you. It'll take three hours to file you two apart, so's I'll be on the train when you leave here. You better foller an' ketch me . . . so's we'll have some real fun explainin' in court how come the two of you was handcuffed an' left behind by a pore old feller without any weapons but two hands an' a knee. I'll leave your guns an' your keys with the ticket agent at the railroad. The tin star, though, I'm afeard I'll have to keep with the cat skin an' the china egg an' such like truck that don't mean nothin'. Now holler your heads off gents . . . I'm leavin'!"

Mounted on a shaggy burro — the nearest thing to a horse that the village could produce — Whiskers Beck left San Juan. He disdained to fork his ignoble mount. He sat sidewise, instead, like a man sitting on a log. That way he could better keep his feet from trailing on the ground. Behind followed a second burro, bearing a Mexican boy and Beck's valise.

"Maybe," said the boy as they plodded past the last house, "I should run back after a bottle of something to drink."

"Not much," said Whiskers, leisurely making a cigarette. He hitched one of his gun belts into a more comfortable position. "Can'tcha see I'm fleein' fer my life?"

ABOUT THE AUTHOR

Alan LeMay was born in Indianapolis, Indiana, and attended Stetson University in DeLand, Florida, in 1916. Following his military service, he completed his education at the University of Chicago. His short story, "Hullabaloo," appeared the month of his graduation in *Adventure* (6/30/22). He was a prolific contributor to the magazine markets in the mid-1920s. With the story, "Loan of a Gun," LeMay broke into the pages of *Collier's* (2/23/29). During the next decade he wanted nothing more than to be a gentleman rancher, and his income from writing helped support his enthusiasms which included tearing out the peach-tree orchard so he could build a polo field on his ranch outside Santee, California. It was also during this period that he wrote some of his most memorable Western novels, *Gunsight Trail* (1931), *Winter Range* (1932), *Cattle Kingdom* (1933), and *Thunder in the Dust* (1934) among them. In the late 1930s he was plunged into debt because of a divorce and turned next to screenwriting, early attaching himself to Cecil B. DeMille's unit at Paramount Pictures. LeMay continued to write original screenplays through the 1940s, and on one occasion even directed the film based on his screenplay.

The Searchers (1954) is regarded by many as LeMay's masterpiece. It possesses a graphic sense of place; it etches deeply the feats of human endurance which LeMay tended to admire in the American spirit; and it has that characteristic suggestiveness of tremendous depths and untold stories developed in his long apprenticeship writing short stories. A subtext often rides on a snatch of dialogue or flashes in a laconic observation. It was followed by such classic Western novels as *The Unforgiven* (1957) and *By Dim and Flaring Lamps* (1962).